THE SEVEN DEADLY SINS

Seven Scars They Left Behind

Stories by Shuka Matsuda
Created by Nakaba Suzuki

Translated by June Jungreis and Maria Maita-Keppeler

VERTICAL.

Prologue

A time before the human and nonhuman worlds were separated.

Before giants and fairies disappeared and became myths—when they lived side by side with humans.

When magic and martial power were intertwined.

There were soldiers who still possessed within themselves magic that most other humans had lost—when was it that they came to be known as "Holy Knights"?

It was said that one Holy Knight boasted the strength of a thousand ordinary knights; they became part of the saying, "Where there is a kingdom, there are Holy Knights; where Holy Knights are naught, no kingdom shall be." By then their fame was acknowledged by all.

In the Kingdom of Liones, the most powerful in all Britannia, there was once a legendary order of Holy Knights who were deemed the strongest in the land.

The order brought together seven savage criminals, and they came to be known as the Seven Deadly Sins.

Christened with the names of the seven sins that lead people to ruin, each member of the order was believed to possess tenfold the magical and martial abilities of ordinary Holy Knights. However, there were many mysteries about their origins. Some were so mysterious, no man had ever seen their faces.

Their strange origins, coupled with the endless secrets surrounding them, made their very existence fit to be called a living legend.

However—
One year, on the morning of the kingdom's anniversary festival, they suddenly betrayed the kingdom.

They brutally slayed Zaratras, the Captain of the Holy Knights, and then fled, evading the pursuit of the entire Holy Knight army. They henceforth hid away somewhere and became fugitives.

But someday, perhaps they will return...

Perhaps their betrayal was the beginning of the Prophecy of the Holy Crusade—that legend passed down since antiquity, of a great battle between light and darkness...

At least, there were those who whispered such rumors.

However, there were two people who knew the truth behind what happened that day.

The secret was too big for the two, still young and innocent, and it consumed them and tore at their minds. But for ten long years they would do their best to bear it in silence.

This is the story of one summer during those ten long years.

The story of a beautiful princess and her faithful knight, and the people who knew them.

The story of the seven scars that the Seven Deadly Sins left behind when they fled.

C O N T E N T S

CAST

Gilthunder

Holy Knight apprentice,
son of slain captain
Zaratras

Margaret

First Princess of the
Kingdom of Liones

Griamore

Holy Knight apprentice,
nephew of Zaratras

Howzer

Holy Knight apprentice,
son of blacksmith

Veronica

Second Princess of the
Kingdom of Liones

Elizabeth

Third Princess of the
Kingdom of Liones

Hendrickson

One of the two Holy
Knight Captains

Vivian

Apprentice of "Boar's Sin
of Gluttony" Merlin

The Seven
Deadly Sins

Chapter One
The Princess of Sorrow and the Minstrel's Song
—*from Escanor*

The bright full moon shone quietly on the surface of the lake.

A small island floated in the middle of the lake, and on it, an old castle stood leaning over the edge of a tall cliff.

The castle was made up of a snug keep with living quarters and two towers. Lights shone from several windows.

Faint laughter could be heard, and it seemed that even past midnight, the residents of the castle were still not asleep.

The shadow of a man loitered atop the rampart connecting the living quarters with the First Tower.

The man had a tall, thin build and was wearing clothes that were much too baggy for him. The features of his slightly oval face were well put together, in their own way, but his stooping posture and unconfident expression ruined them.

"Hahh," he sighed, leaning on the edging along the top of the wall.

His gaze had been fixed on the tower to his right for some time.

A light flickered in the window on the top floor of the tower. The man had been staring at the light, but after a while he turned his eyes away and sighed again.

Looking down from the rampart, he could see the sandy beach that spread out on the other side of the lake. It stood out palely in the moonlight.

"'The beach suspended in moonlight is like your pale white arms. Coming in and out of sight in the dark waves, revealing the truth'..."

He muttered the mysterious words, then let out a self-deprecating laugh. "Search as I might, I guess someone like me could never find the words to express her beauty and kindness and intelligence."

He looked up again at the First Tower.

"Oh, but I wish I could...Merlin."

1

The Kingdom of Liones, extolled as the strongest country in Britannia.

Surrounded by a city wall to guard against attacks, the royal capital sparkled in the dazzling morning sunlight.

It was June; the nights were short and the dawn broke early each morning. Most of the people were still asleep.

In Liones Castle, which looked down on the capital, the bedrooms of the royal family, too, were all quiet and still.

The king's oldest daughter, Princess Margaret, nearly fifteen, lay in bed clothed in layers of silk and lace.

However, her beautiful face was strained with anguish.

Her white hands gripped the bed sheets, and her lips trembled. Her mouth opened as if to scream, but made no sound, and shut tightly again.

It was as if she were holding back, even in her sleep.

Margaret was dreaming.

It was a dream about two years ago. A dream of that terrible morning.

She was in a room in the old castle on the outskirts of the royal capital. In the room was a man's corpse, drenched in blood.

The corpse had been pierced by innumerable spears and swords, and now hung in the air.

His beautiful silver hair and golden armor were stained a deep red.

His bloody feet floated above the floor. *Plip. Plip.* Blood dripped down from them and spread out across the stone floor.

Margaret held her hands over her mouth and stifled a scream.

She had to keep herself hidden. If she were discovered, it would be the end for her.

Two figures stood in front of the mutilated corpse of the Captain of the Holy Knights.

Two men who should not have been there, who *could* not have been there.

They were huddled close together, discussing something.

Pale cheeks. Margaret could just barely hear their words.

"Yes—this should do."

All that was left was to wait for the Seven Deadly Sins…

"...!"

Margaret awoke with a start.

She was covered in sweat.

She slowly sat up in bed and steadied her breathing. From the light slipping through the curtains, she realized that it was already morning.

I should get up, she thought. At the same time, a brisk knock sounded against the door to the dressing room attached to Margaret's.

"Princess Margaret. Good morning. It's me, Grace." The voice sounded troubled.

Grace was one of her lady's maids. She was probably worried that Margaret hadn't gotten up yet, even though it was past time to.

"Your Highness?"

With a click, the door opened a crack. Margaret caught a glimpse of Grace's red hair.

"Don't come in!" Margaret shouted reflexively.

"Ah—a thousand pardons!" The door closed in a hurry.

Grace was a new lady's maid who had come to the castle just that spring. She was only fifteen, the same age as Margaret. Today was her first day helping with Margaret's morning routine, and perhaps her mistress' sudden scolding had given her a shock.

Even so, Margaret had a reason for not wanting Grace in her bedroom.

Yes—and it wasn't just Grace. Margaret didn't want her other lady's maids, or her sisters Veronica and Elizabeth, or even her father the king to come into her room.

She never wanted *anyone* to enter.

At that moment, the lace canopy of her bed swayed, though there was no wind.

Margaret flinched in surprise.

"Get away," she whispered bluntly. The lace swayed again.

An invisible presence—something dreadfully large was staring at the bed.

"Don't come near!"

There was the sound of something dragging. That *thing* must have been moving away from the bed.

Slowly, sluggishly, making that faint dragging sound, the *thing* moved toward the edge of the room. When it reached the wall, its presence disappeared.

Margaret shivered.

She hadn't seen its physical form since that day two years ago. But she had always known that the horrendously creepy thing was lurking nearby.

It wasn't a creature of this world. It was a grotesque monster born of sinister magic.

It was a fearsome guard that had kept watch over Margaret ever since she bore witness to that secret two years ago.

Doing her best not to look at the corner of her room, Margaret got out of bed. Even though she couldn't see it, just knowing it was there made her feel sick.

The monster had shown its hideous true form once, and the

sight was still etched in the back of her eyelids, even now.

Eyes that stuck out to the left and right; a body shaped like a giant slug; the wings of a bat…

Margaret shivered again, then shook the memory from her mind.

She slipped on a lace shawl hanging on a nearby chair and gently opened the door.

Grace was sitting on the sofa in the corner of the dressing room. She looked up when she noticed Margaret coming in, but was wringing a handkerchief tightly in her hands, and her eyes were red.

"Oh my, Grace, are you all right? Did I speak too harshly?" Margaret hurried over to her lady's maid.

"No, no, it's not your fault, Your Highness. I've just got something in my eye…" Grace nervously tried to explain it away, scrubbing at her eyes with the handkerchief.

Margaret knelt down in front of Grace and grabbed her hands to keep them still. "Don't rub so hard. You'll hurt your eyes."

"Don't—Your Highness, please don't kneel." Looking shocked, Grace took Margaret by the arm and tried to make her stand.

But Margaret shook her head. "I really am sorry, for shouting at you. I had a frightful dream before I woke up, and I was all worked up about it."

"My, was it really such a frightful dream? Now that you mention it, Your Highness is covered in sweat…"

"Oh, is it that bad? But I'm fine—it was just a dream." Margaret touched her hand to her forehead and made herself smile.

from Escanor

"But, Your Highness, they say nightmares forewarn illness. And I've heard they can also be a sign of an evil magician's curse."

Margaret's breath caught at the word "magician."

But she quickly smiled again.

"Oh, I'm sure it's nothing like that. Sorry for worrying you. Anyway, please help me get dressed, or I'll be late for breakfast." Margaret took Grace by the hand and pulled her up from the sofa.

"Y-Yes." Grace finally smiled, too, and stood up with a swish of her short braid.

2

"...and that's what happened, Erica."

That afternoon, Grace was walking down a corridor in the castle alongside Erica, another one of Margaret's attendants. Since Grace had had the early shift, she was wearing plain clothes now, but Erica was wearing her aproned maid's uniform.

"Hmm...that's happened to me, too." Erica was only two years older than Grace, but she had been in the service of the princess for over five years. "Or perhaps I should say, these past two years, it's happened several times... Princess Margaret has changed a bit."

"She's changed?"

"Yeah. She used to be more cheerful. Then again, a lot has happened since then."

"What do you mean?"

"Well, there's what happened to Lord Zaratras, for one."

The moment the name left Erica's lips, a soldier walking down the corridor a little ahead of them glanced back with a start. Erica quickly faked a smile, then lowered her voice. "You know about it too, right? How Lord Zaratras, the previous Captain of the Holy Knights, was killed."

"O-Of course."

There wasn't a single person living in Liones' royal capital who didn't know about it.

There had been a tragedy two years ago, on the morning of the kingdom's anniversary festival. Zaratras, at the time the Captain of the Holy Knights, had been brutally murdered in the old castle on the outskirts of the capital.

It was said that a single Holy Knight possessed the martial and magical power of a thousand ordinary knights. The captain who governed over all of those Holy Knights must have been unimaginably strong.

That such a personage had been atrociously murdered would in and of itself have been a major incident, but what was more, the offenders were the members of the Seven Deadly Sins—an order of knights who were well trusted by and served directly under the king.

But the Seven Deadly Sins, just seven people surrounded by all of the kingdom's Holy Knights, had broken through the ring, shaken off pursuit, and escaped. Their whereabouts were still unknown.

"Captain Zaratras was an old friend and trusted subordinate of His Majesty the King, so to Margaret, he was like a favorite uncle. She and young master Gil, Captain Zaratras' son, were practically like siblings," Erica said, taking the opportunity to show off her seniority.

Grace tilted her head. "When you say Gil, you mean Lord Gilthunder, the Holy Knight apprentice, right?"

"Yep."

Even Grace knew Zaratras' son Gilthunder. A boy with reddish-brown hair and good features, he stood out among the apprentices training to become Holy Knights. "Was he close with Princess Margaret?"

"Yes, he was. They grew up together. He was like her personal bodyguard, you know? Even though the young master is a year younger." Erica continued with a ribald grin. "This is just a hunch, but I'm sure Captain Zaratras and His Majesty the King must have considered the possibility of setting the two up for betrothal! Young Gil would succeed his father and become Captain of the Holy Knights, and Princess Margaret would become the Queen of Liones… Romantic, isn't it?! Like it was meant to be?!"

She got excited as she talked, and her voice rose again. When Grace frowned at her, Erica just laughed, *Tee hee,* pretending not to notice.

"The two of them don't seem quite so close now, though," Grace pressed, to which Erica sighed.

"That's true. You could say young Gil completely changed after his father was killed. He used to be a cute little boy, open and cheerful and a bit of a crybaby."

"Wow…"

"But it's not just those two, though. Ever since then, His

The Seven Deadly Sins

Majesty the King is often melancholy, and the whole castle has gotten gloomier. We keep getting nothing but more of the most boorish soldiers. Lord Dreyfus and his lot all seem tense somehow, too."

Dreyfus was the late Zaratras' younger brother. After the incident, he assumed his older brother's role as Captain of the Holy Knights. He was an earnest man and, not believing himself to be fully ready to act as captain, received special permission from the king to share the position with his good friend Hendrickson.

"Which is probably because they know that those backstabbing Seven Deadly Sins could always return—they can't let their guard down against a group of such heinous villains who scattered all the Holy Knights with just seven people. In the end, it just goes to show that no matter how strong they were, gathering criminals to form an order of knights wasn't a good idea."

They reached the rear entrance of the castle.

"Your house is on…Birch Street, right?" Erica asked.

"Yes."

"I'm heading in that direction too, so let's go together. I've got to pick some things up at the sundries shop on Birch Street."

They pushed open a small wooden door and came out into the West Garden, where a refreshing breeze was blowing across the greenery. Summers were beautiful in Britannia.

"…Ah, speak of the devil—it's young master Gil." Erica pointed discreetly. Grace looked over as well.

Toward the edge of the garden, several young soldiers and knights seemed to be engaged in some sort of training. Some were sparring with swords, others were pointing at and discussing the rampart around the garden. The boy with the pretty face who stood out among them was Gilthunder, son of the late Captain Zaratras, and Princess Margaret's childhood friend. One year younger than Margaret, he would turn fourteen this year, but he looked rather grownup for his age.

One of the young soldiers noticed Erica and Grace walking through the garden and whistled at them, teasing. Erica, apparently an acquaintance, stuck her tongue out mockingly in return. It roused a laugh out of the group.

But Gilthunder alone, straight-faced, turned his gaze elsewhere.

When Grace absently followed his line of sight, she was surprised by what she found.

Gilthunder was looking at the tower built into the west wing of the castle, all the way across the garden.

Grace could see a figure in the tower's small window. *Princess Margaret...*

Her long platinum-blond hair was unmistakable even from far away. She was wearing the dark blue dress that Grace had helped her into that morning.

The princess was staring straight back at Gilthunder. Her expression was unreadable from the garden, but there was no mistaking that she was looking this way.

A crow on the castle wall cawed hoarsely. As if the call had reproached him, Gilthunder broke his gaze away from Margaret.

Grace hastily averted her eyes as well.

"Hmm? Something the matter?"

"No, it's nothing."

When Erica cocked her head, Grace just smiled reassuringly. She felt like she shouldn't share what she'd just seen.

The pair continued out the castle's west gate and down into the surrounding town.

"What will you do for the Summer Solstice Festival? Are you working?" Erica asked as they walked along the brick road.

The summer solstice was next week, on the 22nd of the month. Various festivities were held around the castle town to enjoy the longest day of the year, starting on the 21st and lasting for three days.

"No," replied Grace, "they let me excuse myself from duty starting the afternoon of the solstice. My older sister, who moved to Vaizel when she married, is coming home to visit and bringing her child, so I'd like to go see a play with her."

"Wow, sounds nice. I took the day off, too! Oh, look, they've already set up some of the stalls."

Just as Erica said, decorating and preparations for the festival had already begun. Liones Kingdom banners hung from the eaves of the stores along the main road. Some shopkeepers had set up tables in front of their stores, where they were selling special sweets and clothes and odds and ends that people would need while preparing for the festival.

"'In celebration of Princess Elizabeth's birthday,' it says."

In front of a confectionery shop, a stand adorned with a portrait of Princess Elizabeth was selling bags of candy. The 12th of that month had been the third princess' birthday. Representing

her age, this year the little bags held nine pieces each.

"It used to be that starting from Princess Elizabeth's birthday, lasting through the solstice, and on until Princess Margaret's the next month, a stream of visitors would come to the castle; it was very lively. But that stopped two years ago like everything else." Erica let out a long, disappointed sigh. "These days the talk at the castle is all wretched and nothing bright. Ghosts popping up and such."

"What?!" Grace inadvertently shouted. Erica shushed her.

"You haven't heard? They say Princess Margaret is being haunted by some sort of ghost."

"What—why...?"

"Well, in the past, the lady's maid on duty in the morning would open Princess Margaret's bedroom door and wake her up. I mean, I had one of the lowest positions, so I was never assigned, but..."

"Is that so?"

"Mm-hm. Back then, someone of your position wouldn't have even been allowed in her dressing room. But that's no longer the case, since there aren't as many lady's maids now."

"..."

"Anyway, two years ago, Princess Margaret suddenly started disliking it when attendants came into her room—even to clean. Now Agatha the head housekeeper does the cleaning alone, and only on days the princess specifies."

Now that Grace thought about it, that was true. A job like that, especially, should have come around to a low-ranking attendant like herself, but it never did.

"People say they've heard the princess sobbing in her room in the middle of the night, or that they've sensed the presence of some sort of big creature. Some of the more fainthearted attendants quit because of it. If the princess were her old self, she surely would have kept them from leaving. But even when Clara, who had been in her service for quite some time, said she was resigning, the princess just said, 'I see,' and let her go."

"But…what would want to haunt Princess Margaret?"

"That, I don't know. It's just a rumor, after all. I've never seen the thing." Erica cackled. She herself didn't seem to believe it. Grace was slightly taken aback.

"You're fond of stories like that, aren't you, Miss Erica."

Erica didn't seem to mind the comment at all, even coming from her junior. "I love 'em! I mean, stuff like this is what makes working at the castle so fun!"

Something in the distance caught her eye and she pointed. "Oh, look! The minstrel is here! He's sort of good-looking, isn't he?"

A cluster of about a dozen people had gathered in the small square up ahead. In their center, a young man sat on a curb, strumming a lute.

"Ah, it seems more young ladies have come by. In that case, I think it's time for a love song."

The minstrel spotted Grace and Erica immediately as they joined the little crowd, and sent them a playful wink. Erica squealed and waved.

The Seven Deadly Sins

"You're too kind, miss. Now then…let's see…" he said while nimbly tuning the strings of his lute. "I found this poem hand-written into a book I purchased here in the capital of Liones, when I was passing through for the Summer Solstice Festival last year. I don't know who wrote it or where it's from, but for some reason it touched my heart, and I decided to give it a melody. If by some chance any of you fine citizens know who wrote it, I would be much obliged if you could tell me. Now then…"

And with that, he started to sing.

A clear, resonant tenor flowed from his perfect lips. "'The beach suspended in moonlight is like your pale white arms. Coming in and out of sight in the dark waves, revealing the truth'…"

The beach suspended in moonlight is like your pale white arms
Coming in and out of sight in the dark waves, revealing the truth
The shadow of the mountains reflected in the lake is like your noble profile
It wavers in the light and wind; I stretch out my arms but I cannot reach

This lone old palace on its tiny island feels like a stone cell that holds me bound
My body is cursed and torn apart by the fates of the day and the night
It stands here still as stone, it sighs

Oh, that I might be allowed just to sing about you here
Though my hands might never touch you and my voice you never hear
Because standing here remembering you and singing your praises
Is the only thing that I can do

from Escanor

"How dreamy…" Erica said, spellbound. The rest of the women in the crowd looked charmed as well, all listening with rapt attention.

Grace, too, had closed her eyes and was lost in his voice.

But for some reason, what appeared in her mind was the scene that she had witnessed earlier.

The princess and her beautiful knight, separated by a hundred feet, gazing at each other for just a moment.

They had been close childhood friends—perhaps even engaged to be married. What in heaven could have come between them?

It was hard for Grace to believe that they had simply had a falling-out.

Surely, there's some reason. As a lady's maid, she was of course not permitted to pry into her mistress' private affairs. She had been strictly told so when she started service at the castle.

But there must be something—*something* she could do.

Listening to the minstrel sing his love song, Grace sunk deep down in thought.

3

That morning, Margaret woke with tears on her cheeks again.

But it hadn't been a bad dream. This one had been wonderfully happy.

A dream of the past—she hadn't known anything back then.

On my honor as a knight, I'll protect you as long as I live, her kind childhood friend had sworn.

The Seven Deadly Sins

A dream about several years ago, when she childishly believed that her days would continue forever just as they were.

"Gilthunder..." She couldn't resist whispering his name.

When she did, she felt that big presence next to her bed rear its head.

"Oh, shush! Go away! I know!" Was she not even allowed to whisper his name in private? Margaret bit her lip and sat up.

She doubted the monster had any volition or intelligence of its own.

It was just reacting to certain words and people.

Margaret and Gilthunder. The two who knew the secret weren't allowed to seek help from anyone, or comfort each other, or even take their own lives. But this monster wasn't the one who had decided thus—that woman had.

The secret:

That the Seven Deadly Sins hadn't been the ones who killed Zaratras.

They had simply been caught in a trap and wrongfully accused.

And the real murderers were none other than the two who were currently sharing the role of Captain of the Holy Knights.

But even so, there was nothing that Margaret could do.

She took a deep breath, put on her shawl, and, as usual, opened her bedroom door herself, acting as if nothing was wrong.

"Good morning."

"Good morning, Princess Margaret." It was Grace who stood

from Escanor

up from the sofa and bowed her head.

"Hmm? Wasn't Erica on duty today?"

"Yes, she was, but…I asked her to switch."

"Oh? Why?"

Grace smiled vaguely and didn't answer. But once Margaret had sat down in front of the mirror, the lady's maid reminded hesitantly, "It's almost time for the festival."

The Summer Solstice Festival was three days away.

"Mm-hm."

"I heard that Princess Veronica and the others are going with their escorts. Won't you attend too, Princess Margaret?"

"Mmm—I'm not a fan of crowds, so…" Margaret said with a laugh.

Grace's face fell, but she was determined. "Perhaps…would you go with Lord Gilthunder?"

Margaret's breath caught at the sudden mention of Gilthunder's name. She froze, trying to detect that presence. "…Why would I?"

"Er, I heard from Erica that you used to be close."

"That was back when we were children." She was trying with all her might to keep her voice from shaking. She couldn't feel the monster's presence. It probably didn't respond to her lady's maid's voice.

"I haven't even spoken to him in a very long time," Margaret said, keeping her eyes downcast.

Grace opened her mouth, but closed it after a moment without speaking. Instead, she pulled a little folded-up piece of paper from her maid's uniform.

"Um, here."

"…What is it?"

Grace gently closed Margaret's hand around the paper. "A minstrel was in town for the solstice festival, and this is a song he sang. It was so lovely I had to write it down. Your Highness, if you don't mind, I think you should read it too."

Margaret opened up the note with her pale fingers to reveal hastily scribbled lyrics.

It was a love poem that a man had addressed to the woman who held his heart.

"'The beach suspended in moonlight is like your pale white arms. Coming in and out of sight in the dark waves, revealing the truth'…"

Tears welled in Margaret's eyes as she absorbed the words.

—*This lone old palace on its tiny island feels like a stone cell that holds me bound…*

When she read that verse, a particular landscape came to her mind.

Stony mountains, their peaks wrapped in perpetual snow. A lake reflecting them on its calm surface.

An old castle stood on a small island in the middle of the lake, across from a white beach.

Our royal villa in the north…

from Escanor

Years ago, back when Margaret's mother was still alive, they had all gone there on holiday.

Her little sister Veronica had been two or three; her youngest sister, Elizabeth, an infant.

Zaratras and his brother Dreyfus had both come with their families as well.

I played with Gilthunder in that castle's garden and on the beach…

Could the image in this poem be about that same castle?

Or was it just some other, similar place?

Margaret bowed her head and pressed the piece of paper to her heart. Tears drip-dropped onto her knees.

Oh, that I might be allowed just to sing about you here
Though my hands might never touch you and my voice you never hear
Because standing here remembering you and singing your praises
Is the only thing that I can do

Grace handed her a handkerchief and opened her mouth, carefully picking her words. "I hope I'm not being impertinent, but I just wanted to say…there are ways to let him know how you feel, even without meeting in person. Though it's not my place to meddle." She bowed her head apologetically.

Margaret slowly shook her head. "Not at all… Thank you. Really."

Grace is right, Margaret thought.

She had felt as though she and Gilthunder were little birds

trapped in two separate, invisible cages.

They would gaze at each other from far away, meeting each other's eyes only for brief moments.

They would hold still and listen whenever they heard the other's voice drifting over from somewhere, making sure to keep out of sight.

And that was all they could hope for. All they were allowed to hope for.

Surely, as long as they kept up their act, *that woman* would think they had drifted apart.

Margaret had already started to resign herself, little by little, to such a fate. She realized that.

But—*maybe there* is *a way to show him that my feelings haven't changed.*

Surely there was. And without being noticed by that woman—or the two Captains of the Holy Knights.

"Thank you so much, Grace," Margaret said, taking hold of her attendant's hand and raising it to her forehead in gratitude.

"You're welcome, but… Please let go of my hand!"

Grace repeated herself several times, embarrassed, but Margaret did not let go.

Chapter Two
The Boy and His Spear

—from King

At dusk, the Black Cat's Yawn was bustling with people taking an early supper.

"Your order, sir!"

A plump, middle-aged woman—she looked like she must be the proprietress—set down a plate on one of the outdoor tables. It was laden with the tavern's specialty: white fish filet boiled with vegetables and topped with melted cheese.

"Thanks."

A pair clad in knight's armor smiled up at her. One of them was a boy with blond hair that stuck out in all directions; the other, a heavy-set adult.

"Looks delicious," said the boy, darting his fork out to skewer the filet.

"Stop that!" said the older man. "This is my order! Wait for your pork sauté!"

"Come on, just a little. You can have some of mine."

"Whenever you say that, Chief, you just take everything! I don't even like pork. Anyway, this one is mine!" The man picked up his plate with both hands and held it above his head.

At the same time, a small black shape pranced lightly off the low brick wall between the seating area and the garden.

"Yikes!"

31

The shape landed for a moment on the man's plate, then hopped nimbly to the ground.

"Augh! Hot, hot, hot!" The man was so surprised he let go of his plate, spilling sauce and cheese all over his head.

"Whoa!" The boy pointed to the floor. "Hey, King, that cat got you good."

The man, King, turned around to find a big black cat. The fish that had been on King's plate a moment before was dangling from its mouth.

"Hey! Give that back!"

"What're you gonna do if you get it back?" the boy said, laughing. "You can't eat it now."

The black cat stared up at King with a *mine now* look plastered on its face.

"A stray cat like this needs to get some sense beaten into it." Furious, King stood up and advanced toward the cat, his face still covered in cheese. But the cat didn't run. On the contrary, it suddenly turned towards him and charged.

"?!"

It happened in the blink of an eye. The cat ran up King's legs and onto his shoulder, forcefully dug its claws into his face, and jumped back onto the wall.

"Aughhh!!" King's scream echoed through the tavern. The other diners, who'd been watching attentively, burst into peals of laughter.

from King

1

About a dozen people were gathered on a stretch of bare, rocky land a mile away from the royal capital of Liones Kingdom.

The majority were young Holy Knight apprentices, clad in light practice armor. They were lined up in a semi-circle observing a boy who stood in the center.

The boy must have been about thirteen or fourteen. He held a club at an angle in front of his face and stared straight ahead with a determined look in his eyes. The object of his gaze was a large boulder resting on the ground, so big that even four adults wouldn't be able to wrap their arms around it.

The boy lowered the tip of his club down almost to the ground and a whirlwind rose up from the spot with a *fwoosh*.

He slowly waved his club, articulating a horizontal figure eight with the tip. The whirlwind gradually grew bigger and started to spin faster.

With a "Hah!" he sent the howling whirlwind—it could easily be called a tornado at this point—rushing straight forward, where it encircled the enormous rock. It shattered instantaneously with a thunderous roar, but amazingly, none of the pieces came flying out of the whirlwind.

"Wow!" the others cheered.

The boy gently lowered his club, and the tornado gradually died down, leaving a mound of pebbles that used to be the boulder in its place.

"Well done, Howzer," called one of the onlookers, a man in

the prime of his life with a splendid physique. He sounded satisfied.

The boy who had been called Howzer turned around, looking proud of himself. "Thank you, Captain Dreyfus!"

"Your control is very good. You used to just strike out at random, but it seems you've matured. Griamore, take note." Dreyfus directed this last remark at his son, who stood diagonally behind him.

The dark-haired boy, who looked like his father, hunched his large body over. "I-I'm sorry, Da—I mean, Captain."

"Well, but Griamore's progress recently has been remarkable as well," Holy Knight Dale gently cut in. Dale was one of the coaches for today's training.

Dreyfus, however, shook his head. "But he's been inconsistent since he was a kid. If a knight can't keep up a stable stream of defense magic, it can prove fatal. You should be working him harder than that. And Gilthunder, this goes for you too."

"Yes, sir." Gilthunder, who stood next to Griamore, lowered his eyes and bowed his head.

"You haven't been progressing as fast as we expected lately. Your swordsmanship is weak. If my brother could see you now, he'd be disappointed."

"Understood, sir. I'll work hard so as not to disgrace my father's name."

"You're too hard on your relatives, Captain Dreyfus," another one of today's coaches, Nicholas, cut in with a laugh. He was a giant who towered over even Dreyfus. "Your son and your nephew have both been doing fine work. This group you saw today is made up of by far the sharpest and strongest of all the Holy Knight apprentices. All they need is some real combat experience, and in one or two years they'll be plenty skilled enough to be called proper Holy Knights."

"Aye." Dreyfus nodded. "They're certainly promising. I'm counting on you to train them well."

Dale and Nicholas gave their captain a sharp salute, then turned back to their young charges. "All right, break up into pairs again. Since the captain will continue to observe us, be on your best performance, everyone."

"Yes, sir!" The Holy Knights-in-training formed into the same pairs as before and spread out across the training ground.

"Hold up, Howzer," Dreyfus called to the boy who had just demonstrated the impeccable wind magic.

Howzer had been about to run off with Gustaf, his training partner for the day, but he froze mid-step, surprised. "Yes, sir! What's up, Captain?"

Dreyfus strolled over to Howzer and apprised the club the boy was holding. "You're still using that?"

"Yes...?"

Most of the Holy Knight apprentices came from families who held knight status, but Howzer, odd one out, was a commoner. The big difference between commoners and knights was that knights were allowed to carry swords in public, while commoners were not. Since Howzer hadn't been officially recognized as a knight yet, he usually used a club or blunt sword during training, too. In contrast Gustaf, though he was the same age as Howzer and stood next to him on the same training ground, was the eldest son of a knight family and had always owned his own real sword.

"That club is no longer adequate for drawing out your magical potential. I hereby authorize you to carry swords. I expect you to come back tomorrow with a real sword to practice with."

"F-For real?"

"Mm-hm." Dreyfus nodded magnanimously. "As a Holy Knight, your weapon is an extension of your body. Each weapon is different, and some will be more suited than others to your magical abilities, talents, and physical build. Think carefully about what will best bring out your strength."

"Y-Yes, sir! Thank you, sir! Wahoo!" Howzer literally jumped for joy, waving his club high up in the air.

2

"Mom! Mom! Gimme the key to the storeroom!"

Howzer was shouting the moment he ran into the shop.

The shop in question was the blacksmith's on the western edge of the capital—Howzer's house.

His mother looked up from where she was wiping down the negotiating table in the middle of the room. "Excuse me, young man?" she admonished. "Don't I even get a 'hello'?"

But Howzer just galloped over to her, paying no heed to her tone. "Mom, guess what? I was acknowledged by Captain Dreyfus! He said I'm allowed to carry a sword!"

from King

"What? Really?!" His mother's eyes opened wide in surprise. "So you...you're really going to be a Holy Knight? It's really possible?"

"'Course it is!" Howzer puffed out his chest. "Being allowed to carry a sword means I'm already on the same level as a knight! I've still got to prove my strength in real combat before I become a Holy Knight, but I mean, that's only a matter of time now!"

"Well, I'll say!" his mother enthused, looking him over as if seeing him anew. "My little boy who used to do nothing but fight every day and never did any chores—I thought you were headed straight down the path to becoming the town outcast. But now you're going to be a Holy Knight!"

"Mom, I get it already! Can I just have the key?"

"The key?" Coming back to herself, his mother reached into the front pocket of her apron and pulled out her ring of keys.

Impatient, Howzer grabbed it right out of her hands. "I'm gonna pick out one of Pops' swords!"

He ran through the shop room in a flash and rushed out through the wooden back gate into the courtyard.

His father Raizer's workshop stood on the far side of the yard. One half of the building, facing the canal that ran along the right side of the yard, was the workroom with the furnace. As always, Howzer could hear the systematic banging of a hammer through the wide-open doors.

But rather than the workroom, Hozwer headed straight for the door on the left of the building. He inserted the key in the lock hanging from the latch and opened the door with bated breath.

Inside was the storeroom where Howzer's father kept the weapons he'd forged. Most of them already had buyers and were just being held temporarily, but some were not.

"Hmm, where is it..." Howzer walked around the storeroom and started rummaging through the shelves.

He was looking for a longsword that his father had forged a few years ago. It had seemed to be his father's pride and joy: Howzer remembered how when he finished the sword, Raizer uncharacteristically called Howzer and his mother outside to show them how well it had come out.

But it had yet to attract a buyer, and it should still have been tucked away somewhere.

"Crap!"

While Howzer was searching the shelves and wooden crates with a bit too much gusto, he accidentally knocked over several spears leaning against the wall. He started returning them to their places, but one of them felt a little strange when he picked it up. He stared at the shaft.

What the... Like it's stuck to my hand...

He opened his palm to check if there was something coating the shaft. But there wasn't.

Just my imagination?

He put the spear back against the wall with the rest of them, then started searching the shelves again.

"Here it is!"

He finally found the longsword he was looking for and pulled the blade from its black leather sheath. Even in the dim light of the storeroom, it shone brightly, as if light were coming from the blade itself.

"Wow, so cool!" He gripped the hilt with both hands and gazed at the blade, transfixed.

Longswords were practically a symbol of the knights. They were his father's specialty when it came to weapons, and what was more, Howzer's idolized Captain Dreyfus was famous for wielding them.

"What are you doing, Howzer?"

Howzer jumped at the sudden sound of his father's voice behind him.

He turned to find his father, drenched in sweat from working. "Pops…"

He almost tried to hide the sword behind him, like he used to when he was caught misbehaving as a kid, but then he remembered himself. Of course, there was no need to be secretive anymore.

"Pops, Captain Dreyfus gave me permission to start carrying swords today. So let me have this sword. All this time, I've—"

"That's not the right weapon for you," his father muttered.

That ticked Howzer off. "What does *that* mean?! Are you saying I'm not worthy of it?"

"I don't care if you use it." His father's face, half obscured by a thick beard, was also being backlit by the sun coming in through the doorway in which he stood, and Howzer couldn't read his expression. His hair, the same golden brown as Howzer's, was shiny with sweat.

"What?"

"I don't care if you use it. If something like that is good enough. Do what you like." His father turned indifferently and ambled away. "Your mother says dinner's ready," he announced as an afterthought, his voice already far away.

3

"Darn it, why won't it work?" Howzer gritted his teeth and glared at the boulder in front of him.

It was the next day. He'd appeared at the training ground, coveted longsword triumphantly in hand, and called his peers over, bragging about how he was going to pulverize a boulder twice as big as the day before, but…

"What the heck?" However many times he tried, he couldn't get the hang of it.

Then again, there was no mistaking that the amount of magic he could release was much higher than what he'd been able to muster with the club. For some reason, though, it felt like it was all leaking out through both edges of the longsword.

As a result, although the whirlwind Howzer conjured was several times larger than yesterday, it was hopelessly scattered. His friends had to run about for cover, and the whole scene had turned into a huge mess.

"Ugh! Why?!"

"Just cut it out, Howzer!"

The training ground was enveloped in thick dust that the tornado stirred up, and stones of all sizes were raining down on their heads. Griamore unleashed his magic wall to shield some of the apprentices; a sphere of light expanded out from where he stood and repelled the wind and rocks.

"Shut it. I'm trying again!"

"Doing it again won't change anything, Howzer," Gilthunder said calmly.

Howzer turned to him with an annoyed look on his face. "What does *that* mean, Gil?"

"It might be the problem." Gilthunder pointed at the long-sword in Howzer's hand. "Maybe it's not a good fit for you."

"…!"

That's not the right weapon for you.

Gilthunder's voice seemed to echo what his father had said yesterday.

Howzer burst out before he could stop, glaring at Gilthunder. "Are you saying I'm not fit to be a knight? Is that it?"

Gilthunder shook his head. "That's not what I mean. It's just…"

A beautiful longsword rested in Gilthunder's hand. It was one that Howzer's father had forged.

Howzer looked at Griamore, who stood across the training ground. The longsword that hung from his waist had been passed down to him from his father, Dreyfus.

Bitter aggravation rose up from deep inside Howzer. "Whatever," he spat. "I'm going home!"

"Howzer!"

Gilthunder and the others all called out his name. But Howzer ignored them, sprinting from the training ground without even looking back.

4

The long stretch of bars and restaurants called Drunkard's Way was even more lively than usual in anticipation of the Summer Solstice Festival next week.

Liones royal banners and summer solstice flower wreaths hung from eaves; food carts and stalls lined the usually bare roadside, and foot traffic was dense. Although the persistent summer sun was still high in the sky, the bells signaling the hour had just struck eight o'clock in the evening. It was already time for dinner.

"Looks crowded in there," Howzer muttered with a sigh. Too upset to go home, he had been wandering aimlessly around the castle town, but now his usual haunt, the Black Cat's Yawn, appeared to be full.

"Oh, is that Howzer?" the tavern's proprietress called out to him as he was peeking through the entrance to check if there were any open tables.

"There aren't any tables, are there, ma'am?"

"Hmm, we are pretty full today. Would you mind a shared table?" She pointed toward the outdoor seating area. Indeed, Howzer could see a girl his age sitting alone at one of the two-person tables.

The girl looked over at them and piped up.

"Oh, Howzer! It's been such a long time."

from King

"What's this now—you two know each other? Well then, go sit down!" Laughing, the proprietress pushed Howzer over to the table and then disappeared back inside the tavern.

"Er…who are you again?" Howzer sat down reluctantly, scrutinizing the girl's face. Her frizzy red hair was pulled back in two short braids. He was sure he'd seen her somewhere before…

"You can't tell? I'm Grace, from the medicine shop."

"Oh, the one on the corner of Birch Street!"

Now he remembered. She was the second daughter of the family that ran the big medicine shop near his house. She was a year older than him. They had played together sometimes when they were very little, but they hadn't spoken at all in the years since, and Howzer had completely forgotten about her.

"I see you around at the castle sometimes," Grace said. "You used to just be a bossy kid but seem to be doing well for yourself these days."

The proprietress herself came by, and Howzer ordered his favorite, roasted chicken thigh. Turning back to Grace, he asked, "At the castle? Are you working there now?"

"Yeah, since this spring. I wait on Princess Margaret."

"Huh. Is Her Highness well?"

Howzer had asked the question casually, but Grace's face clouded over.

"Yes… But, well—Howzer, you've been training at the castle for a while now, right?"

"Hm? Yeah, for about…five years? Maybe a little more." He counted the years on his fingers.

The Seven Deadly Sins

"Is it true that Princess Margaret used to be more cheerful?"

"Uh, maybe? I dunno that much about the princesses. I bet Gilthunder would, though."

"Oh?! Howzer, are you friends with Lord Gilthunder?" Grace leaned forward suddenly, and Howzer was startled by her sudden interest.

"Um, yeah. Kinda."

"Gilthunder also used to be a more cheerful person, right?"

"Huh?" Howzer had no idea why Grace was asking, but he thought over the question anyway. "Now that you mention it, I guess so."

"Do you know what happened?"

"What happened? Well, duh," said Howzer, slightly taken aback. "Who wouldn't react that way to something like that happening to his father? And with the Seven Deadly Sins being the ones behind it—that's not something you just bounce back from."

"Did Lord Gilthunder have some connection with the Seven Deadly Sins?"

Howzer grimaced at Grace's persistent interrogation. "When Gilthunder was a little kid, Meliodas, the leader of the Seven Deadly Sins, used to teach him swordsmanship sometimes. After his own teacher went and killed his father, well, it's no wonder he's lost a little faith in people."

Gilthunder never seemed to want to talk about it, and Howzer himself had always been a bit wary of the famed strongest order of Holy Knights, so the topic rarely came up.

"And I mean, he's always been an overly serious guy. I'm sure

from King

he's just focused on becoming a Holy Knight right now. Maybe so he can avenge his father."

As he was speaking, Howzer thought back to the scene he'd made at the training ground earlier and started to regret his own behavior. He felt embarrassed about having taken his anger out on Gilthunder, who hadn't done anything to deserve it.

"I'm not particularly worried. He's not the sort of guy who messes up," Howzer insisted with some passion.

But Grace just said, "I see," and lowered her eyes, apparently lost in thought.

The proprietress returned with a plate of roasted chicken. "Here you go," she said, setting the plate down on the table.

"Yummm, looks delicious!" Relieved by the change of topic, Howzer reached for his chow.

But then—

A small black shape sprang to life atop the adjacent low brick wall separating the seating area from the garden.

"Huh?!"

A big black cat suddenly leapt down onto the table. It tried to snatch the chicken from Howzer's plate.

"Hold it, you bastard!" Howzer reached out quick as lightning and lifted the cat up by the scruff of its neck. "You have some nerve trying to swipe *my* dinner."

The cat kicked its limbs around wildly, but could do nothing to break free suspended in Howzer's solid grasp.

—*Nice catch, lad!*

—*That stray cat is infamous around here.*

The other patrons cheered raucously.

The proprietress smiled. "Well, well, looks like our stray cat's finally been caught."

"Has it been causing you trouble? What should I do with it?" Howzer held the cat out to her.

"Ma'am, let's off that rascal." A drunk had stumbled over from one of the indoor seats. "That cat's stolen from me way too many times, and I'm pissed. Give it here, boy."

The man's arrogant attitude rubbed Howzer the wrong way. "Hold on. I'm the one who caught it, and this is this lady's tavern. It's none of your business what we do with the cat."

"…d'you say?" the man slurred, growing angry.

The other diners all started chiming in.

—*Yeah, kill the rascal!*

—*No, leave the poor cat alone.*

"Now, now. Calm down," said the proprietress, stepping between Howzer and the man with a chuckle. "This cat has certainly caused us quite a bit of trouble, but after all these years I've gotten strangely attached to him. This tavern is called the Black Cat's Yawn, after all—and he's pretty cute if you actually look at him…"

"I-I agree, ma'am," Grace added from behind. "Um, by the way, I could take him, if you want. He might be able to help with a rat problem back at my house." She tried to scoop the cat into her arms.

But the cat, even dangling in the air as it was, let out a menacing hiss and lashed out at her with both front paws.

"Hey, cool it!" Howzer said to the cat, hastily trying to pull it away from Grace. But Grace just stretched her arms out further.

"Ack!"

While they were going back and forth, Howzer's grip loosened for a moment. The cat saw its chance and twisted right out of his grasp, landing upright on the floor. It shot like an arrow through the tavern and disappeared into the street.

"I-I'm sorry!" Grace said, instinctively apologizing to Howzer, the proprietress, and everyone else in the tavern.

But the drunken patron from before flared up at her.

"What'd you do that for, little missy? Huh?!"

"It's not her fault," Howzer cut in. "I'm to blame for not holding him tighter. If you're going to complain, do it to me." He glared scathingly, and the man backed down, hunching and lowering his eyes.

"Wh-Whatever. It's just one stinking cat..." he mumbled as he hurried out of the establishment.

After a moment, the tension in the tavern dissipated with a collective sigh, and the lively atmosphere returned.

"Maybe this time that cat'll learn to stop messing with everyone's food..."

"Oh, but he's getting old now. He used to be downright uncatchable!"

The regular customers laughed, as did the proprietress.

"That reminds me," she said. "Do you guys remember that Holy Knight a few years back who kept getting done over by that cat?"

"Yeah, yeah! That cat really got him good!"

Another burst of laughter. Howzer and Grace exchanged a look.

"A Holy Knight? Done over by a cat?"

"Yep. He was a heavy fellow, and he was always getting his food stolen by that cat."

"He'd chase it around, but the cat would just mess with him, and he'd usually end up scratched."

"Was he really a Holy Knight?" Howzer was shocked. But the proprietress and the men just guffawed.

"That's what we asked ourselves, too, in the beginning."

"Mm-hm. But that one time was really something…"

"That one time?" Grace asked.

The group of regulars launched into the anecdote together.

"A bad sort of drunk came in one day, right? And after getting into a quarrel with a girl who was working here at the time, he tried to drag her outside with him."

"He was huge, and what's more, he was brandishing a knife, so there was nothing anyone could do to help."

"But then, that fellow who was always getting done over by the cat…"

The regulars described how all of a sudden, the knight leapt nimbly through the air and, with an enormous spear—"I don't know where he pulled it from"—pinned the man to the floor.

"A spear…" gasped Howzer.

If no one had known where it was hidden, that meant it had

been a magical weapon. And if that man had been able to master it, and to fly through the air, he really had been a Holy Knight.

"It was an amazing spear. He said it was what let him unleash his full magical power."

"I guess he meant he wasn't going to use that kind of magic on some cat."

"Even if that's true, though, he was such a klutz without it."

"Wahahaha!" the men all laughed.

"I haven't seen him around lately. I wonder if he went away on some distant assignment."

"Wasn't there a rumor that he was one of the Seven Deadly Sins?"

"He looked a lot like one of the guys on the wanted posters, but his face wasn't so wicked. He was always smiling."

"Yeah. And if he'd been one of the Seven Deadly Sins, he would've been able to best that cat, even barehanded, don't you think?"

That drew another burst of laughter from everyone. But Howzer wasn't listening anymore.

"A spear..."

"Howzer, what's wrong? Your chicken is cold—want me to make you another?"

"Howzer?"

Howzer shook his head absently at the women. He pulled a silver coin from his breast pocket, handed it to the proprietress, and rushed out of the tavern.

5

"Mom! The storeroom key!"

Just like the day before, Howzer burst shouting into the shop. He snatched the keys right out of his mother's hands and made a beeline for the storeroom.

Bursting in, he ran to the wall and grabbed one of the spears that he'd knocked over last time.

"..."

Again, he felt like the spear was being sucked against his hand. He carried it outside.

There was a wide clearing behind the workshop, past the left side of the building. It was standard practice to not build other houses near a blacksmith's, so that in the unlikely event of an accident, neighbors wouldn't be affected.

Boxes full of raw ore and firewood and coal were piled along one edge of the lot. Howzer held his spear ready and fixed his aim on one of the wooden crates.

"..."

Gripping the shaft in his right hand, he could clearly feel the magic spiraling through the spear. It pulled in the surrounding air, which in an instant surged out from the tip and formed into a small whirlwind.

"..."

It felt as if the weapon and his arm had become one. He could see the path that led from the spear straight to the center of his magic.

"Is this the one?"

He raised it over his head at an angle. The small but fearsomely agile whirlwind followed the exact trajectory that Howzer imagined, blowing up small stones in its path, and the crate he was aiming for was smashed to bits in an instant.

"..."

Howzer just stood there for a moment, watching the chunks of ore scatter.

"Is that your answer?"

It was his father's voice.

Howzer turned to find Raizer standing behind him, work clothes covered in sweat. Howzer panicked for a moment, trying to explain himself.

"Sorry for messing up your materials! But—"

"Don't worry about it."

His father slowly walked over to Howzer and touched the spear he was holding. Howzer handed it to Raizer, who inspected the tip with narrowed eyes.

"It's cracked."

"Huh?" Howzer looked too to find that there was indeed a small notch on the blade's edge.

"Weapons are made to suit the individuals who use them. That's especially true for Holy Knights. I'm just a layman's blacksmith, so I can't make the special weapons that high-ranking Holy Knights wield. That's the magicians' domain."

"Pops..."

"And your magic is at that level now."

from King

"Can't I fight with a sword that you made?" Howzer said, but then startled at his own words.

Somewhere along the way, he had convinced himself that fighting with his father's sword would earn his approval.

His whole life, Howzer had been nothing but defiant, running off to do his own thing with no intention of taking over the shop, and he'd thought his father hadn't forgiven him. Howzer must have unconsciously thought that using his father's sword would redeem his irresponsible childhood and that his father wouldn't approve of his choices otherwise.

But his father broke into a satisfied smile behind his beard. "You've become a fine young man, Howzer. Surely Captain Dreyfus or His Majesty the King will find a spear for you."

"Pops…" Howzer stared dumbly at his father for a moment, then suddenly reached to remove the sword at his hip. "Y-You can have this back."

"No, you keep it. Maybe you'll never use it in battle, but a knight should always have a sword at his waist."

Raizer turned his back and returned to his workshop without a second glance.

Howzer watched his father's receding figure. After a moment, he placed his hand on the sword at his hip and let his face, which looked just like his father's, fall into an embarrassed smile.

Chapter Three
A Recipe She Could Not Crack

A peculiar smell hung about the room.

The built-in shelves and table in the center were filled to bursting with mysterious objects.

Old books. Bones of unfamiliar creatures. Bottles of sinister-hued liquid. Pots that rattled from time to time. Stones that gave off a faint glow.

In addition, blades and spearheads and other weapons. Pieces of armor. There were shoes and gloves as well.

Bundles of withered plants hung from the ceiling. Dried snakes and lizards and the limbs of other beasts poked out through the leaves.

Most likely, these things were also exuding considerable odors of their own, but the smell that filled the room at the moment came from the steam wafting out of the large, simmering cauldron mounted next to the wall.

It smelled a bit like food, a bit like medicine, or a bit like something slightly rotten. It changed on every inhalation, and "peculiar" was the only way to describe it.

A beautiful woman stood before the cauldron. Dark gray hair hung about her shoulders, and she had bright amber eyes. She tossed another big apple into the pot.

A cloud of steam spewed out of the cauldron, and for a

moment, a tart, sweet smell drifted through the air. But it soon mixed in with the original odor.

"An apple, a peach—and then a double-headed fish, ten pounds of pork, the blood of a clay dragon..." she muttered to herself, writing something down on the sheaf of papers beside her. After a moment, she put down her feather pen and held both hands out above the cauldron.

"..."

As an incantation spilled from her red lips, too quiet for an ordinary person to hear, the liquid in the cauldron busily changed color and bubbled up—*blub blub blub*. Something appeared to be forming inside.

The woman inspected it and then held her right hand, fingers together, just above the surface of the liquid.

A brown lump about the size of a walnut rose up from the cauldron with a faint splash. Without hesitation, the woman took a small pot from the shelf to her left and scooped up the lump from where it floated in mid-air.

"Hmm...I suppose this should do for now. I'll have to make a few more and test them."

The woman breathed a sigh of relief as she covered the pot.

Then she looked back over her shoulder.

"Don't just stand there peeping—if you're going to come in, come in, Vivian."

The door to the room clunked and then, after a moment, slowly opened.

A young woman with an awkward expression on her face

appeared in the doorway. "Please excuse me. I brought that thing you asked me for."

"I appreciate it. Put it over there."

The woman called Vivian put the basket she was holding down on the table.

The other, beautiful woman inspected it, then turned back to the cauldron.

Vivian glared at her back with jealousy and envy in her eyes, but the woman did not turn around again.

1

A lone female figure walked down the pitch-black passage, holding aloft a small lantern.

The narrow passage was barely wide enough to fit two people walking side by side.

Judging by the bare rock walls and floor, it was a cave of sorts that had been dug into the ground.

The woman's face was hidden behind an oddly shaped mask, and she held a long staff in her left hand. A giant ornament shaped like a human left hand was affixed to the tip. No, but the nails were sharpened to a point, so perhaps it was the hand not of a human, but of a monster.

As the woman walked, the passage gradually widened, until it suddenly opened out into a spacious cavern.

The frail light that she held was not strong enough to illu-minate the recesses. The far edge and ceiling stayed lurking in darkness.

But she could clearly sense the presence of something alive in the room.

And not just one. Many, many creatures.

The smell of animals and dung filled the air. Grimacing under her mask, the woman slowly lifted her lantern and surveyed the cavern.

Many cages stood against the wall.

There were large ones, small ones, and even some that could be cradled like birdcages.

Creatures were imprisoned in them according to their respective sizes.

An enormous eagle. A gray bear. A lion that must have been brought in from the southern continent.

There were chickens and pigs as well. Sand lizards. Scorpions. Poisonous spiders.

"You're late, Vivian."

A lantern lit with a whoosh on the far side of the cavern, revealing a tall man. His bluish-gray hair was cut short and he sported a goatee, but he wasn't that old. He looked to be around thirty or so.

"Were you with Gilthunder again?"

"That's none of your concern, Hendrickson," Vivian retorted hotly.

Hendrickson barked a short laugh. *True,* it seemed to say. "Anyway, how is that thing doing?"

"Well…it seems calm, for now."

from Merlin

Hendrickson held the lantern in his left hand out toward the back of the cavern. Vivian aimed her own lamp in the same direction.

The two lights shone on an especially sturdy-looking cage.

A large beast crouched inside.

Its back was covered in glittering green scales, and a line of horns sprouted along its spine and down to its thick tail. Wings, made of membrane stretched across talons, sprouted from both sides of its back.

The ten-foot-long creature appeared to be an infant dragon.

However, from its belly up, the scales were replaced with a gray bristle that covered the front half of the creature. Its forelegs were the paws of a beast, not the claws of a dragon.

Its slobbering head turned atop its thick, maned neck. From its enormous, sword-like fangs, it was clear that the monstrosity was part sword wolf.

Its long tail jutted out from a gap between the bars and swayed back and forth sullenly.

"Here is where the problem starts." Hendrickson gripped a small needle in his right hand. "Subdue the creature," he said, approaching the monster's tail.

Vivian put her lantern down at her feet and placed both hands on her staff, then turned back to the monster.

She started muttering a spell under her breath, which caused the creature to freeze in place.

Slowly, but purposefully, Hendrickson stuck the needle between the scales on the thick tail before using his thumb to crush

the sphere attached to the end of the needle.

The monster's tail twitched.

Hendrickson stepped back swiftly, returning to Vivian's side. "Well?"

"It's no good," Vivian said, lowering her staff. As soon as she did, the monster let out a piercing shriek. The roar rumbled and echoed around the cavern, and the animals in the surrounding cages started to panic and rage.

Thrashing its head and limbs about, the monster destroyed its cage in an instant. Its body started to expand rapidly—like water filling a leather bag, or a giant swamp frog's bulbous throat.

"Get rid of it," Hendrickson said coldly.

Vivian nodded. "Perfect Cube," she chanted, and a cube of light formed around the monster. The raging monster grew bigger and bigger inside the cube until finally, with a dull pop, it turned into a square mass of flesh.

Vivian silently waved her staff. The lump of flesh and the cube of light both vanished somewhere.

"Hmm… It just won't seem to work," Hendrickson muttered.

Vivian shrugged. "I wonder if it's a problem with the amount of Demon's Blood?"

"Or maybe it's because your fusion magic is underdeveloped."

"Oh!" Vivian said discontentedly. She removed the mask that had been covering her face, revealing the features of a simple young woman. Her curly, light brown hair was plastered against her forehead with sweat. "My chimera was perfect. Do me a favor, don't point fingers. Aren't you being too greedy? You seem to have bought up another batch of animals from the circus."

"Greedy or not, there's no use discussing it now. We must create something that, if not in all aspects, at least in combat power, is stronger than any of the Seven Deadly Sins."

"You make it sound easy, but certain combinations of animals are more compatible than others." Vivian raised her eyebrows. "If you match animals helter-skelter just because they're formidable in battle, their power will conflict and the creature will become unbalanced."

"Hmm…would your mentor say so, too?" Hendrickson laughed disparagingly.

"Wh-What?" Vivian gasped.

Hendrickson laughed down his nose at her again, then left the cave without another word.

2

"Nkk… Just you watch!!"

Vivian clenched her teeth in front of a huge pile of books and papers.

She stood in a room in Hendrickson's magical research hall. The hall was built on an enormous, oddly shaped rock that towered just northwest of the center of the royal capital of Liones. It had originally belonged to a member of the Seven Deadly Sins: Merlin, the Boar's Sin of Gluttony, who was hailed as the most powerful witch in Britannia.

"Definitely somewhere around here…"

from Merlin

As Vivian rummaged across the desktop, a whole mountain of books collapsed in a flutter. A startled meow came from near her feet.

"Oh, did I surprise you? Sorry." Vivian searched for the source of the sound.

A large black cat crouched under the desk, looking up at her. There was fear in its eyes.

Maybe the spell isn't working right.

She had picked up the cat a little while ago down in the castle town. It had run out right in front of her and seemed like it might scratch her, so she had promptly cast some charm magic on it…

Vivian squatted down and recited the spell once again. The cat's eyes became unfocused for a moment, and then it started to purr.

"Nice kitty." Vivian stroked the cat's head, then returned to looking over the desk.

There were quite a few books filled with Merlin's handwriting. They were all concerned with animal fusion. Vivian had searched the library and the bookcases in all the rooms in the building and gathered them together here.

"I won't be outdone by that woman anymore. I've studied and I have the practical experience now."

Vivian opened a record of some fusion experiment that Merlin had been commissioned by the king several years ago. Merlin had of course made no effort to reveal what she was creating to Vivian, merely her disciple, but Vivian remembered some complicated fusion magic experiments that involved not just animals, but plants too.

"What does this mean? I don't understand this description. Is it in an ancient language? It's not a rune, and I've never seen these words before…"

She hurriedly flipped through several other books—herbological encyclopedias and dictionaries for the languages of dead cultures.

"I don't understand…" She bit her lip. "The answer couldn't possibly be in one of those books we sold off…right? No, there's no way."

Vivian pushed down the twinge of unease that had risen in her chest.

Two years ago, Hendrickson and Dreyfus had conspired together to pin the blame for Captain Zaratras' murder on the Seven Deadly Sins. After they had driven the Sins from the capital, Hendrickson took over this hall, which used to belong to Merlin. When he did, he and Vivian, his magician collaborator, had thoroughly ransacked the building and disposed of everything they deemed unnecessary.

They had thrown out or sold a countless number of books, but none of them had had any relation at all to magic. They hadn't even belonged to Merlin—mostly, they were personal belongings that other members of the Seven Deadly Sins had left lying around.

"I checked those all over carefully—there's no problem there," Vivian assured herself.

There were certain fixed rules when it came to genetic splicing. Ignoring them and forcing combinations resulted in chimeras that couldn't live very long and that fell short of the original animals' potential.

"If it can't be done, then it can't be done!" she fumed. But Hendrickson's words drifted through her ears again.

Would your mentor say so, too?

"How frustrating!"

She screeched like a child and threw the nearest book down onto the floor.

The cat jumped again and hissed.

3

"Good evening, Gil."

When Vivian teleported into Gilthunder's room, she found him sitting at his desk reading some sort of document.

"Hey, Vivian."

Gilthunder turned to her, smiling thinly. Vivian knew it was a fake smile, but she pretended not to notice.

"What were you reading?" Vivian leaned coyly against the boy and reached for the document on his desk.

"The schedule for during and after the Summer Solstice Festival break."

"Huh…"

Vivian glanced at the document. It appeared to be a schedule, just as he'd said.

"So…what are you doing for the festival, Gil?"

"Umm…nothing in particular."

The Seven Deadly Sins

Vivian was lost in the beauty of his downcast profile. He really was such a lovely boy. He had stood out since his early years, but recently he had gotten more manly, too, and now he was positively radiant.

Vivian knew that every smile he showed her was forced.

Even so, she wanted to keep him in her grasp.

She would do anything for that. Anything at all.

Though it was all lies now, if they continued spending time together like this, surely his heart, too, would someday be hers.

Vivian narrowed her eyes. Gilthunder looked away uncomfortably.

"Hey, Gil. Want to go to the festival together?" Vivian proposed.

Gilthunder's eyes widened for a moment, and then he seemed to give it some thought.

"…Unless you'd rather not with me?"

"Sure, I'll go." Gilthunder faced her with another forced smile.

"Oh, good! All right, I'll come pick you up tomorrow evening!"

4

Just past nine in the evening, dusk was finally starting to settle over the long, long day of the summer solstice.

The sun hid behind the western city wall, and lamps were lit here and there about the capital. Lanterns burned in front of shops, and torches and braziers in street corners, all illuminating the royal banners and festive flower wreaths. The number of people strolling around town showed no signs of dwindling, and laughter spilled out endlessly from the restaurants and taverns. Children who were allowed to stay up late just for tonight ran about, stuffing their mouths with baked sweets from the stalls. Young people were dolled up in their very best outfits, and many an arm was linked with a sweetheart's.

A round of partner dancing had started in the central square. A lottery to pair up single dancers with partners bustled along with it.

The sea of lovers danced around to the tune of a jaunty waltz. Vivian watched them from the corner of her eye as she and Gilthunder walked along the edge of the square.

"Is there anything you want to see, Gil? I heard the circus this year is excellent," Vivian said, pointing to the large, recently pitched tent that took up the northern half of the square.

"Yeah, I think Howzer and the others went to check it out." Gilthunder nodded, glancing at the tent.

"Are you interested? Shall we go, too? I heard a dragon pup is going to jump through a ring of fire."

"Nah." Gilthunder shook his head, eyes downcast.

"Well then, do you want to get something to eat? Apparently the stall over there is pretty good…"

"Uh huh." Gilthunder looked up at the sky, where the edges of the sunset were slowly starting to turn purple. At about the same time, the bells signaling the hour chimed out ten o'clock. "They're selling fish that are wrapped in pie dough and fried, aren't they?

I'll buy some for us. You can—oh, how about you wait over there and listen to a song?"

"Ah, really?" Vivian brightened and clasped her hands in front of her despite herself.

"I think they've got sweet sauce and savory sauce—tell me again which kind you like?"

"I'll take the sweet one."

Vivian couldn't believe that Gilthunder was going out of his way to be nice to her. With high spirits, she watched him walk off, then headed toward the western end of the square like he'd told her to.

The area had been turned into a small stage for minstrels and street performers.

A raised platform had been built into a recess of the square, and wooden benches were lined up around it in semi-circles.

When Vivian arrived, a beautiful female singer had just finished her act and was trying to step off and away from the stage, showered with cheers and applause. A ten-year-old boy—he was probably her apprentice, or perhaps her son—held out a hat and weaved through the spectators, collecting tips.

Next up, a youthful man ascended the stage. He was rather handsome and carried a lute in his arms; he winked at the young ladies sitting in the front row. A handful of men left their seats and were immediately replaced by flocking girls.

Vivian sat down on an unoccupied two-person bench near the edge of the semi-circle and waited restlessly for Gilthunder to return.

from Merlin

Meanwhile, the young minstrel finished tuning his lute and cleared his throat.

"I'm so glad I could come again this year to Liones Kingdom's tradition-steeped Summer Solstice Festival. May you all have the chance to dream for at least a moment this short summer night."

The young ladies fluttered with excitement at his smooth voice, so perfectly matched to his handsome face. Vivian looked over her shoulder and finally saw Gilthunder walking back with something wrapped in paper in both hands.

"And now, for my first song—a maiden I met the other day requested that I absolutely sing this first today. Is the young lady here, I wonder?"

The minstrel made a show of looking across the crowd.

"Hmm, she doesn't appear to be… But perhaps she is listening somewhere. Or maybe she's gone to summon her sweetheart?"

Laughter spilled from the audience.

"Gil, over here." Vivian waved discreetly, and Gilthunder padded over and sat down next to her. He gently set the paper-wrapped pie in Vivian's hand.

"Thank you." Vivian ducked her head and blushed slightly. Maybe after this, if she invited him to the lovers' dance, he would be so kind as to oblige her.

The minstrel picked up his lute again and began to pluck the strings in a cascade of notes.

"I have no intention of prying boorishly. I hope that my song might touch your hearts," the minstrel said. He took a deep breath, and at last started to sing resonantly.

The Seven Deadly Sins

The beach suspended in moonlight is like your pale white arms
Coming in and out of sight in the dark waves, revealing the truth
The shadow of the mountains reflected in the lake is like your noble profile
It wavers in the light and wind; I stretch out my arms but I cannot reach

This lone old palace on its tiny island feels like a stone cell that holds me bound
My body is cursed and torn apart by the fates of the day and the night
It stands here still as stone, it sighs

Oh, that I might be allowed just to sing about you here
Though my hands might never touch you and my voice you never hear
Because standing here remembering you and singing your praises
Is the only thing that I can do

"What a nice song." Vivian, enthralled by the performance, looked at Gilthunder beside her.

When she did, she was taken aback.

Gil?

Gilthunder was weeping.

Or rather, he was biting his lip trying not to cry, but tears he couldn't hold back were gathering in his eyes.

Gil…

The moment Vivian saw this, she felt her heart grow suddenly cold.

It was certainly a good song, and maybe for a young woman it would make sense, but she couldn't believe that it was moving

from Merlin

enough to make a fourteen-year-old boy—to make Gilthunder—shed tears like this.

His hands trembled minutely, and he hadn't taken even one bite of the pie that he had bought.

Oh, that I might be allowed just to sing about you here
Though my hands might never touch you and my voice you never hear
Because standing here remembering you and singing your praises
Is the only thing that I can do

The minstrel sang the last verse again and again, and then he gently stilled the music from his lute.

Applause erupted with *oohs* and *ahhs*. The minstrel took his brimmed hat from his head and handed it to a girl in the front row. She tossed in a silver coin and passed the hat to the next seat.

"And for my next song…"

This time, a slightly faster, cheerier song began. The lingering applause turned into people clapping along to the beat.

However, Vivian wasn't listening anymore.

What had the minstrel said just now?

A maiden I met the other day requested that I absolutely sing this first today.

And yet the one who requested it hadn't shown up.

But perhaps she is listening somewhere. Or maybe she's gone to summon her sweetheart?

…summon her sweetheart…

The Seven Deadly Sins

Several images churned through Vivian's head.

Gilthunder had looked up at the sky earlier, as if confirming the time signaled by the bells.

What if—what if he had come here today specifically to listen to this song?

Was that why he'd accepted Vivian's invitation? Was that why he'd bought her food?

Was it all so that he could come here at the right time?

That implied only one answer.

Margaret!

Of course. That girl.

The platinum-blond girl who lived always in Gilthunder's heart.

But—but how?

Vivian shrewdly turned over the possibilities.

She had set the greatest chimera she'd ever made to stand guard over Margaret. It was a monster that constantly monitored the girl's every move while staying under cover, never revealing itself. It would automatically attack Margaret if Gilthunder or anything that smelled like him ever got too close.

And it was the same for Gilthunder. When Vivian herself couldn't be near him, a raven infused with her intentions kept watch over him.

Vivian was sure the two of them absolutely knew all that. In fact, as far as she could tell, for the past two years, they hadn't spoken at all aside from polite conversation in formal settings. They'd shown no hint of exchanging letters, either.

from Merlin

Letters…

With a start, Vivian realized—

The training schedule that Gilthunder had been looking at yesterday.

What if something had been concealed within it?

And if whoever had given it to Gilthunder hadn't been Margaret or one of her attendants?

If it was a training schedule, he probably got it from one of the Holy Knight instructors or fellow apprentices. I've never looked into something like that.

A scene flashed bright into Vivian's mind.

The day I picked up that black cat…

The tavern that the cat had run out of.

When she had peeped inside, Howzer the Holy Knight apprentice had been arguing with another customer.

It hadn't interested Vivian, so she had left soon after, but…she thought maybe he had been protecting some girl.

Right. A young woman with her red hair done in braids.

Now that she thought about it, she'd seen that girl somewhere before, too…

Oh—she's Margaret's new attendant!

Were they friends? Or had they just met there at the tavern?

Howzer was a childhood friend of Gilthunder's but had always been simple, never doubting his preconceptions. He'd never once questioned Gilthunder's change in demeanor, despite being such close friends.

What was more, he respected Captain Dreyfus from his heart,

and Vivian didn't think the boy would even dream of the possibility that Dreyfus and Hendrickson had already betrayed the king.

I was careless to think so...

Precisely because he thought nothing of it, he would agree readily if Margaret's attendant asked him for a favor.

Vivian clenched her fists tight. The nails she'd buffed and painted pink for the date bit into her palms.

"Gil. I'm not feeling well. Let's go home." Vivian pulled heavily on Gilthunder's arm.

His face had completely cleared by then, and he looked at Vivian in surprise, mid-bite into his fried fish. "What? But—"

"Come on. We're going home!" Vivian pulled him forcefully by the arm and stood up. Her untouched pie fell with a plop onto the ground.

5

As soon as she returned to her room in the magical research hall, tears began to spill from her eyes.

"Ugh...sniff... A fool...everyone keeps making a fool out of me!"

When she stomped over to the table, a sudden voice hissed strangely. The black cat puffed up its tail under the table. It also flattened its ears behind its head, completing the threatening posture.

"..."

The charm's effects had worn off.

from Merlin

Vivian had never been very good at mind manipulation magic in the first place. Especially not on humans, but even with animals like cats and dogs, it only lasted for a few days at best.

Looking around, she saw that objects all over the room were knocked over and scattered about the floor. The magic must have worn off while Vivian was away, and the cat had rampaged about, wanting to go outside.

"..."

Her lips trembled.

It felt like someone was telling her there was nothing she could do.

Nothing was going like she wanted it to. Nothing.

Not even this cat would love her. When the magic wore off, it went right back to the way it was.

Vivian waved her right arm. Her staff appeared in her hand. Raising it, she faced the cat and recited a teleportation spell.

"I won't forgive any of you! Mark my words!"

The cat disappeared instantly. Then, as if chasing after it, Vivian did too.

Chapter Four
The Three Sisters and the Curious Puzzle
—from Gowther

Even in the middle of the night when the entire royal capital slept, a few lights yet burned in one hall, in the laboratory that belonged to the mistress, or perhaps, from the merrymaking of late-night visitors.

Sometimes, a Holy Knight arrived hidden from the eyes of the public to pick up secret magical gear.

Which windows were illuminated, and when, depended on the day.

There was one room, however, that every day—from dusk to dawn—never went dark.

Tonight, again, light leaked from it.

That room, where each and every wall was occluded by bookshelves, appeared at first glance to be some kind of archive for the witch who owned the hall.

If one looked carefully, though, most of the books stashed on the shelves weren't the illustrated guides or scholarly tomes that a witch would need. Most of them were beautiful fables—books of transcribed stories.

Night after night, the occupant of that room passed the long, dark hours absorbed in those stories. After all, he didn't have any need for sleep.

Because of the strange fate bestowed upon him, he always

kept his body covered in a huge suit of armor and a helmet. He only removed them and exposed his naked face to the air for those few hours in the dead of the night in his own room.

Today, too, he sat at the table placed in the center of the room. Before him, however, was not his usual reading, but a dozen pieces of paper.

"Hey, Gowther—what is that?" Merlin the witch, the mistress of the hall, poked her head through a crack in the door as she passed by.

"It seems to be a puzzle," the young man called Gowther answered without turning around.

"Hmph." Merlin entered the room and peered over the sheets that Gowther had spread over the table.

"The Holy Knights were going wild over it, so I borrowed it."

"Ah, that's right, recently it has been popular in the castle town." Merlin slid her finger over the pieces of paper. They were filled with all kinds of things, from word plays to number patterns, from easy problems that even children could solve to complex masterpieces.

"I don't understand what is so interesting about this," Gowther said, tilting his head to the side. There was no expression in the gold irises behind his glasses.

"I imagine you'd think that." Merlin smiled. "With your calculation abilities, I'm sure you can figure out the answers at a single glance—"

"There was a man who said he couldn't solve it for the life of him. He looked so troubled, yet when I told him the answer he threw a fit of rage. Why?"

"He wanted to find it for himself," Merlin said with a laugh. However, it seemed Gowther didn't understand.

"Why go through the trouble of being bothered? I understand people working hard to realize their goals. But where is the profit in suffering to solve such a thing? I heard there's some prize, but is that what they want?"

"How should I explain…" Merlin thought for a moment with a faint smile on her lips, but eventually spoke as if she remembered something. "I know, Gowther, if you find them to be so dull and easy, why don't you try making them?"

"Making them?" Again Gowther tilted his head.

"Yes. Establish a degree of difficulty, come up with a subject, and choose the hints. I think it would be rather interesting," Merlin said. *Right,* she muttered. "While you're at it, maybe I'll have you hide my research findings in a puzzle."

1

In the central tower of the royal castle, a small figure scurried up the stairs with frenzied footsteps. With closely cropped strawberry-blond hair, at first glance it looked almost like a boy. Yet the slender neck and thin limbs were unmistakably those of a young girl.

Her name was Veronica.

Having turned eleven a month earlier, she was the Second Princess of the realm.

"Father! I have to tell you something!"

Without even knocking, she burst through the door into the living room of her father, the king.

"What's wrong, Veronica? So early in the morning…" From inside the room, which was plain for a king's, emerged Bartra. His ample beard was amusingly disarranged from sleep.

"Father. Is it true that sister is moving to the royal villa in the north?"

"Ahh…" King Bartra's face clouded over as he nodded. "She said she wanted to go to a quiet place because she has been in poor health recently."

"It didn't…it didn't seem like she was that ill! Besides, if she's sick she has to see a doctor or a magician!"

"Well, she doesn't want to do that, either… Anyways, please just be kind. She is at that age. She must have something on her mind."

"Big sister is going far away?" Suddenly, there came the voice of another young girl.

Both King Bartra and Veronica whirled around. A small shadow stood at the entrance of the room.

"Elizabeth!"

"Ellie!"

It was Veronica's sister and two years her junior, the Third Princess Elizabeth.

"But it's almost big sister's birthday. I'd hate not to celebrate it…" Elizabeth said with teary blue eyes. King Bartra knit his brow in distress.

from Gowther

Veronica pressed as if it was her only chance. "Then at least shouldn't you assign plenty of knights to guard her? Griamore said Gilthunder isn't going."

"That was also Margaret's own decision. As for her guards, I'm thinking about that as well, so you mustn't worry."

"When will big sister be able to return home?" Elizabeth asked, sniffling. King Bartra smiled.

"That too will depend on Margaret herself... For now, simply see her off."

"I don't want to. I'm sad. Please, father, I want to go too. Please let me go." Elizabeth covered her face and broke out in sobs at last.

Veronica spoke as well. "I must go too. I'll bring Griamore and Gilthunder with me. Why shouldn't I?"

"I can't allow that, Veronica," King Bartra said decisively.

Veronica faltered at the stern face of her father, who was usually so kind.

"You are the Second Princess. While Margaret is gone, you have to carry out the duties of a princess in her place."

"But, at least Gilthunder—"

"Margaret said she doesn't need him—so Gilthunder understands."

"..."

Veronica bit her lip and looked down. Commanded by the king, and not by her father, the girl had no choice but to withdraw.

"Okay... Let's go, Ellie."

Pulling the hand of the still sobbing Elizabeth, Veronica left the room.

The Seven Deadly Sins

After watching them leave in silence, King Bartra slowly turned his back on the doorway. He crossed the room and stepped up to the window on the other side. He looked up at the beautifully clear sky and sighed deeply.

"Margaret...I'm sure it's hard for you right now, but please bear it," the king murmured in a voice that almost completely disappeared in his mouth. "Someday there will come a time when both you and Gilthunder will be requited... The 'Golden Demon' will surely save you both..."

What was it that the king's eyes and their clairvoyant Vision saw?

Not a single soul knew the answer.

2

"Ahh! Goodness, I'm so angry!"

Veronica suddenly punched Griamore in the back as he walked in front of her.

"Ouch! Please stop, Lady Veronica." Griamore looked back with a scowl.

Knowing full well that her blow hardly affected Griamore, who was training daily as a Holy Knight's apprentice, Veronica began to pummel his back even harder.

"Shut up! Oh, father and sister Margaret are so stupid!"

"That hurts—it does hurt."

"Sister, you're hurting poor Griamore," Elizabeth said, furrowing her brow slightly.

from Gowther

Veronica pouted her lips. "But I can't let it go!"

"I don't think hitting Griamore is going to help..."

The three of them left the royal castle and began to walk aimlessly through the capital.

If the king forbade it, there was nothing more they could do. The two princesses gave up on traveling with their big sister and instead decided to search for a parting gift.

"Let's find something perfect together."

"I know... But today isn't the best day." Veronica scratched her head and looked around.

Two days earlier, the Summer Solstice Festival had ended, and now a languorous air floated through the royal city. The ferment of the festival's final events had still lingered the day before, but today, everyone was resting. Particularly at that moment in the early afternoon, it seemed everyone was napping.

Some stores announced their closure for the day, flower wreaths still on display. Other stores were cluttered with remains from a few days of celebration.

Almost all of the myriad of carts and booths that had been lined up in the central plaza were gone.

"Huh?"

At the northern end of the plaza, a large tent was being dismantled. The roof covering had been removed, exposing the structure. For whatever reason, several knights and soldiers were loitering around it.

They surrounded a small, aging man. It seemed he was frantically protesting, but the knights grabbed him and in moments his hands were tied behind his back.

"That man… He's bad?" murmured Elizabeth.

Ah, Griamore said, clapping his hands. "That's the owner of the circus that was performing there. He was arrested during that uproar."

"What do you mean?" asked Veronica, to which Griamore somewhat proudly puffed out his chest.

"On the night of the Summer Solstice Festival, a monster escaped from the circus and attacked some people. It was dreadful. You haven't heard about it?"

"How scary. That happened? When?" Elizabeth's eyes widened.

"It was after dark, after you and Lady Veronica returned to the castle."

"And…why do you seem so happy?"

Prompted by Veronica, Griamore eagerly explained, "In truth, it was Howzer and I who got that monster."

"Wow!"

As Elizabeth gazed up at him with shining eyes, Griamore got only cockier.

"After I escorted you to the castle, I was wandering down a path—you know, the one close to the magical research hall, when I ran into Howzer. And we talked about having a bite together and started toward the plaza when…"

Apparently, a black shadow suddenly jumped out from a back alley and threw itself upon several women who were walking in front of the pair. Hearing their screams, Griamore instantly protected the ladies with a Wall spell, while Howzer flung the beast

from Gowther

away with a Tempest.

"The monster looked like a cross between a black cat, a snake, and things I didn't even recognize… It must have been some kind of chimera made by a magician."

"A chimera… I've never seen one." Elizabeth tilted her head.

"You don't need to! It's a monster made with demon magic!" scolded Veronica.

"Sister, have you seen one?"

"I haven't…"

As they spoke of such things, the circus owner, flanked by soldiers on his right and left, was taken away from the plaza. *I don't know, I had nothing to do with it,* they could hear him protesting even at that point.

"Well, well, that guy doesn't give up easy," someone said right next to them. Veronica and the others turned around to face the man who'd spoken.

"Ah, Sir Dale." Griamore stood up straight and greeted him. It was one of the Holy Knights who also instructed the apprentices.

"Ho, Griamore. And Your Highnesses, are you shopping?" Dale politely greeted Veronica and Elizabeth. Despite his large frame, the toned one of a Holy Knight, his narrow eyes were smiling and gentle. A young girl about Elizabeth's age who stood beside him clutching many books against her chest bowed shyly.

"Are you off today, Sir Dale?" Griamore asked.

Dale smiled. "Yes, because yesterday I was tapped for the whole day to apprehend that circus. It's hard being a low-rung Holy Knight. I'd promised my daughter, and somehow I managed to get today off." As he spoke, he looked at his daughter, who squirmed in his shadow. Her narrow eyes looked just like her father's. "It seemed the owner of that circus was trading in illegal goods on the side."

"Illegal goods?" asked Griamore.

"Drugs, tools that hold evil magic, cursed gems—items generally banned from commerce by the kingdoms of Britannia. Well, most circuses do it. This time as well, they fooled the eyes of the gate guards and smuggled in all sorts of goods."

"I see. I went to see the performance, but...I don't know if I saw anything that looked so shady."

"Aside from their public show, they were offering exhibits in exchange for special fees and making black-market sales. A startling number of sword wolf pelts and fangs were uncovered. They must have taken out an entire pack. In addition, some people reported seeing a fairy clan corpse. If that's true, it's a disaster."

"Fairy corpses!" Elizabeth clung to Veronica in astonishment.

"Please excuse me, Princess," Dale quickly apologized. "That was unpleasant news for you to hear. When we investigated earlier, we didn't see anything like that in the show's cargo, so it could have been a mistake. Of course, we'll be investigating any purchases that might have been made—but anyways, there's nothing to worry about now."

"Father." Dale's daughter pulled the hem of his shirt with slight impatience. As she did, the books that she had been holding fluttered to the ground.

"Oh! Are you okay?" Elizabeth knelt down with the young girl and helped her pick up the books.

"Thank you very much," the girl said bashfully.

Elizabeth smiled as she handed one of the books.

"It's beautiful."

"Yes. I just had my father buy it for me." The girl looked up at Dale happily.

He, too, smiled and nodded. "The bookstore over there opened its back storehouse and they're selling plenty of rare books. Guila likes books so much she just insisted she had to go there today."

"Father." The little girl called Guila tugged at her father's shirt again.

Well then, Dale said his goodbye and left with her.

After watching them go, Elizabeth clapped her hands together and looked up at Veronica. "Sister, I think Margaret also likes books. I'm sure she'll be bored all alone at the north villa. I wonder if a book would be a good present?"

3

"Veronica, Elizabeth, welcome."

Elizabeth stood from the sofa where she had been sitting and smiled at Margaret, who opened the door and entered the living room. As for Veronica, she just couldn't manage to give a proper smile and kept her eyes on the floor.

In her lilac dressing gown, Margaret slowly took a seat on the couch across from them. "I was planning on leaving tomorrow, so I'm glad I got to see you one last time."

The Seven Deadly Sins

Elizabeth's face darkened. "What do you mean, 'last time'?"

Veronica's eyes shot up. "Sister, please rethink this. Is it true that you're only bringing three maids with you?"

"Yes, because they all have their own lives here. I'm sure a few of them will go to you and Elizabeth, so please be kind to them."

"Why…"

Veronica was about to question her again but shut her mouth. She saw clearly that no matter what else she said, Margaret would not change her mind, so firm was the resolve in her eyes.

"Sister, here." Veronica pulled five or so books from the cloth bag at her feet and brusquely placed them on the oak coffee table. "From Ellie and me. The north villa is in the middle of nowhere. We thought you might be able to pass the time with these."

"Wow, thank you." Margaret picked up the first book in the pile and opened it.

Elizabeth leaned forward. "That one! I chose that one! Aren't the pictures beautiful?"

"Yes, they really are. This is scenery from the mountainous region in the north, isn't it?"

It was a beautiful book of etchings. Margaret narrowed her eyes and flipped through the pages with her slender fingertips, but stopped and tilted her head.

"Hmm…"

"What's wrong?" Elizabeth peered in.

"The pages are stuck together here…" Margaret slid in the nail of her index finger and separated them with a light crinkling sound. "Good, I just fixed it… Hm?"

from Gowther

Gently, a sheet folded in half fell from between the pages.

"Huh...I wonder what it could be." Margaret opened it on the table.

"Is it a...puzzle?"

"So pretty—I thought it was a design for a mosaic." Elizabeth also widened her eyes.

Just as she said, it looked like some kind of schematic made up of many small squares. But written in them were a host of tiny numerals, and next to the drawing was a header: *Hints.* Underneath it were a series of closely packed sentences with numbers before each one.

"Does this mean there's a connection between the numbers in the sketch and these 'hints'?"

Veronica looked closely as well. "Ah...are you supposed to fill it in with the answers to the hints, with the first letters starting on the numbered squares?"

"What beautiful letters. It's like a calligraphy manual. I wonder if it was made by the former owner of this book—oh!" Margaret noticed a sentence written in slightly larger lettering at the bottom of the page and read it aloud. "'The one who solves it all shall kiss the witch and gain an invitation to the banquet'..."

"I wonder what it means. Perhaps you understand once you solve it."

"Look, this hint! It says 'the King's three daughters'! Is that us?" Elizabeth said, pointing at one of the sentences.

"'3, 25, 32 are the King's three daughters'—wow, you're right."

"There are nine letters for 3...so perhaps ELIZABETH...25

and 32 are both eight letters, so we don't know if it's MARGARET or VERONICA."

"Oh, but on 26, which is right after 25, it says 'Large, ferocious wyrm,' so 'T' for Tyrant Dragon. So it's Margaret, isn't it?"

"Right—oh, it says 20 is 'The King's magical power.'"

"Father's magical power? Um...if I remember correctly...Vision?"

"'Holy Knight Captain'—is that Dreyfus? Or Hendrickson?"

"—It's Zaratras," Margaret called out the name nostalgically.

"But I don't really get the rest. What is 'Name of lake'? Which lake is it supposed to be? How many lakes do they think there are in Britannia?" Veronica flicked the puzzle with her finger.

Margaret tilted her head. "Hey, Veronica, where did you get this book?"

"At a bookstore on Mimosa Road."

"Apparently, they'd just gotten it out from the back of the storehouse," Elizabeth said.

"Then it was probably made over two years ago—I wonder if it was sleeping in the storehouse this entire time."

Margaret opened the book once again, to where the puzzle had been inserted. A beautiful landscape rendered with the fine touch characteristic of etchings filled an entire page: distant snow-capped mountains were reflected on a shimmering lake, and on a small island on its surface stood a castle.

"I think it's...the north villa," Margaret remarked, surprised.

"Oh, you're right." Elizabeth pointed at the corner of the page. "It says here: 'The Royal Villa of King Liones.'"

"The north villa—as in where you're about to go, sister?"

"Yes. When you and Elizabeth were little, you visited once as well. Don't you remember?"

"No…" Veronica said, before murmuring, *Oh.* "That 'lake' earlier, is that this lake?"

"Maybe it is. I think its name was—Lake Grau." Sure enough, it fit perfectly in the puzzle.

"I see, so the fact that it was inserted by that page was another hint!"

Veronica and Margaret exchanged glances. Both of them looked much more cheerful than before. For whatever reason, they found this very funny and broke out in laughter at the same time. Elizabeth stared blankly up at her older sisters' faces.

"I'm sorry, sis, I won't be so selfish anymore."

"Thank you, Veronica." Margaret smiled. "For now, please let me do as I wish without asking why… I'll make sure to finish this puzzle at the north villa."

"All right. When you do, send a messenger. Then Elizabeth and I will come see you together."

"Yes—I promise," Margaret said. With that, she returned the puzzle to its place, hugged the book, and grinned.

Chapter Five
His Cuisine and the Answer to the Secret
—from Ban

"—What a pain! Why do I have to do this?" a hulking man complained, his silver hair spilling over his shoulders as he shook an iron frying pan with one hand.

"The loser of the bet has to do whatever the other says. That was the deal."

The kitchen was considerably large and splendid, but it looked terribly cramped thanks to the man, who stood almost seven feet tall. Moreover, another stately figure, a woman, was directing him on all manner of things.

That wasn't all.

"Wait, Ban. What kind of meat did you just add?"

The top half of a frightfully large armored knight was poking in from the doorway that connected the kitchen to the backyard. He seemed unable to fit his whole body into the room.

"Huh? It's the meat of a gray wild rabbit."

"In the recipe, it's supposed to be a pulled rabbit."

"There are none around here. So instead ♪" The man called Ban didn't rest his hands as he spoke in his singsong voice. He roughly chopped a yellow fruit, skin and all, and began to pulverize it with a marble mortar and pestle.

"Is that a cirin fruit?" the woman asked.

Ban nodded and said, "Yup, you got it ♪"

from Ban

"Wait, Ban. That's also more than the recipe calls for," the armored knight objected again.

Ban responded with irritation. "The Chief likes it. Besides, gray wild rabbits have a stronger flavor than pulled rabbits, so it's perfect if you add a little more cirin."

"I see." The woman nodded to herself and jotted something down. The armored knight twisted and leaned forward so that his palm almost touched the ground as he followed Ban closely.

"Wait, Ban, that spoon is different from the one you were just using. That's less than precise."

"You're nagging me about everything! It fell on the floor and disappeared somewhere. It's about the same size, so it's fine! Hey, Merlin, send away that bullshit armor. I can't work like this," Ban complained to the woman at his side.

But Merlin only laughed. "Oh, don't say that. It's part of my research. I need Gowther's impeccable memory."

"Heh, do whatever you wish, then, and I'll do the same. Either way, stop commenting on every single detail, Gowther."

"Sure." Gowther lifted an armored finger to signal his assent. *Hmph,* Ban snorted, and without giving the knight a second glance, resumed cooking, humming a tune.

1

Margaret let out a sigh and got to her feet. As she carefully opened the window, the wind blew into the room with a whoosh. She could smell water.

The Seven Deadly Sins

She was at the royal villa of King Liones, which stood upon a small island that floated in Lake Grau. Margaret had been staying there for about a week. It was a terribly quiet place. The closest town was over five miles away, and untamed hills thick with brush completely surrounded the lake.

She was in the highest room on the third floor of the castle, which jutted out from the cliff on the northern side of the island. Directly below her window was the cliff that continued down past the wall, and below that spread the lake's surface. All she could hear was the wind and waves lapping against the shore.

The lake reflected the dull gray of the clouds. The opposite shore was blurry as if it was only a shadow.

"'The lone old castle that stands upon the small island is like a stone cell that imprisons me'—" Repeating the lines that her attendant Grace had heard, Margaret sang in a tiny voice. She didn't know if the melody was correct. "'My body is cursed and torn apart by the fates of the day and the night. It stands here still as stone, it sighs'…" Rustled by the strong wind, Margaret's long platinum-blond hair danced.

"Lady Margaret!" Just at that moment, Grace, who had entered the room, rushed to her side, her face pale.

"What's wrong, Grace?"

"Well, for some reason I thought that you were going to fall…"

"Oh dear, I'm fine."

Grace peered out the window, trembling. "No matter how many times I look, it scares me. The wind is so cold, it'd be better

from Ban

if you shut the window—"

"Right." With a faint smile, Margaret closed the window.

Grace knelt upon the floor to pick up a fallen piece of paper. "Your Highness, here."

"Thank you."

It was that puzzle. It had probably been blown by the wind.

"How are you faring with it?" Grace asked.

"Yes, well…I have a little bit more to go." Margaret smiled, but in her mind, she had begun to give up.

"The hints, they're too sparse… Like, I don't know what you're supposed to do with an obscure one like 'Fish'… 'Put in a rabbit stew'? Doesn't seem like carrot would be the right answer."

"Yes…"

As Grace said, the ten empty spaces that remained corresponded to hints that were far too simple. Margaret was at a loss. She lacked the knowledge to tease out the answers from the connecting words.

"I thought I would be able to help with something like 'Herb'… I apologize for not being more useful." Grace, whose family ran a medicine shop, hung her head.

In the capital, Margaret might have asked somebody about the hints or looked them up in a book—there may have been some way. But all she had at the royal villa was herself, her three maids, and several servants. She could do nothing.

It can't be helped. Margaret closed her eyes. She'd promised her younger sisters to send a messenger upon solving the puzzle, but that seemed unlikely now. *But it's probably for the better. This way, no one will be hurt...*

Margaret glanced at Grace, who was still looking at the puzzle and shaking her head.

The maid suddenly turned around. "My apologies, I'd forgotten what I came for! Your meal is ready."

"All right..." Margaret followed her out into the hallway and spoke to her as they descended the stairs. "Grace, it might be about time that you and Erica returned to the capital. When the next carriage arrives, have it take you on its way back."

"What are you saying?" Grace turned around with a sorrowful expression. "I don't know about Erica unless I ask, but as for me, I will always stay by your side. I was told to by my parents as well."

"But..."

"Um, did I...commit some blunder?" Grace asked, wringing her hands at her chest.

Margaret shook her head from side to side. "It's nothing like that. It's just..."

It's just that you might be put in danger again—Margaret swallowed those words.

Margaret had heard the very next morning from her maid, Erica, who loved gossip, that a monster had escaped from the circus and attacked people on the night of the Summer Solstice Festival. Learning that one of the people who had been assaulted was none other than Grace, she understood everything.

Apparently a chimera, a creature begat with magic, had gone after Grace. In that case, it was the doing not of some circus curiosity, but of that woman—Vivian.

from Ban

Encouraged by Grace's words, Margaret had entrusted her maid with a message, but shouldn't have.

If it was only a date, a time, and a place, she could conceal a message in the Holy Knight apprentices' daily schedule. If the person who gave it to Gilthunder was Howzer, nobody would be suspicious, or so Margaret thought, but that woman wasn't so easily deceived.

Undoubtedly, the chimera that watched Margaret was, even now, hiding somewhere in this castle. Just like back in the capital, it was monitoring her.

To get away from Gilthunder, and to protect Grace, she'd come to the royal villa. Yet Margaret was gradually growing unsure about the best course of action.

2

Crash!

Grace, who had finished hanging laundry in a corner of the courtyard and was resting on a nearby bench, jumped at the loud noise.

She also heard a young man's voice: *You've gotta be kidding me!*

It came from the back door of the kitchen. Grace timidly approached it and peered through the small crack in the wooden door.

A young, blond man wearing an apron was holding his head with both elbows on his workbench. Potatoes and other vegetables still coated in dirt were scattered about on the bench and the floor.

The Seven Deadly Sins

"What more can I do?!" The man then placed his hands on the rim of a shallow bucket in the sink next to him. Grace could see fish swimming inside. It seemed he aimed to flip the bucket over.

"Stop, please stop!" Without thinking, Grace rushed toward him and grabbed his arm.

"Wh-What are you doing?" Caught off guard, the young man whirled around in surprise. "Y-You're the princess' maid…"

"Yes. I'm Grace. Um, what's wrong? Vegetables aside, if you throw the fish out, they'll die…"

"So what if they did," the young man spat, turning away. "Because no matter how painstakingly I prepare her meals, your princess won't eat, will she? Who knows what kind of extravagant fare you serve at the capital…"

"That's…that's not it!" Grace shouted, taken aback. She gripped her apron dress firmly. "The princess came here to recuperate! It's not her fault that she can't eat much!"

"I know that! That's why I'm constantly trying to figure it out. What's nutritious, what has light flavoring, what's easy to eat, what isn't too hot—but it all comes back hardly touched. I'm losing my motivation." The man laughed humorlessly. "Why would she ever bother with the cuisine of a country cook like me? She should have just brought a chef with her."

"Y-You're wrong!"

"What am I wrong about? Really, you call it recuperating, but she didn't bring a doctor or a healer. Are you sure she's not faking it?"

"Wha—" He had gone so far that Grace was left speechless.

from Ban

The man didn't know—just how much Margaret was suffering.

"Her Highness is n-not that kind of p-per..."

Grace started to speak but couldn't continue. She was no different in failing to understand Margaret's suffering. When the man asked Grace why he was wrong, she couldn't explain. She could only repeat that he was wrong.

"Her Highness is..." Tears began to well up in the maid's eyes. In moments, they began flowing and dripping from her cheek to the floor.

"Whoa, hey...don't cry!"

The young man began to panic as if he was just coming to his senses. He restlessly scanned his surroundings, grabbed a yellow fruit that was lying on the kitchen counter, scrubbed the dirt from it with his apron, and thrust it toward Grace.

"I'm sorry I ran my mouth... Here, I'll give you this."

"..."

Grace, who had lifted the hem of her apron to wipe away her tears, was a little appalled. She wasn't a child of five or six, but he seemed to think that a piece of fruit would make her feel better. When she glowered at him with upturned eyes, the young man faltered.

"No, really...I apologize."

"Never mind about me. I can't forgive someone who speaks ill of Her Highness."

"I understand. Sorry—please take this back to your room and have it with the princess. She can stomach at least a little bit of fruit, can't she?" the man said, pushing the gift into Grace's hand.

Accepting it helplessly, Grace tilted her head. "This fruit... What's it called? It's like an apple..."

"Ah, cirins are only picked in this region. They also taste like apples but are somewhat sweeter. You can crush it and add its flavor to a stew too."

"Cirin..." Grace suddenly remembered something. "This must be..." She spun, fruit in hand.

"What is it?!" the young man shouted in surprise, but she didn't bother.

3

"Your Highness! This is it! The cirin fruit!"

Margaret had moved the table up against the window and spread out the puzzle. She was sitting chin in hand when Grace burst through the door and startled her.

"What happened, Grace?"

"I figured it out! The hint! The 'put in a rabbit stew' clue!" Grace, who was normally calm, pushed the yellow fruit at Margaret with uncharacteristic fervor and pointed at one of the blank spaces in the puzzle on the table. "Here! This is 'cirin fruit,' isn't it?"

"Ah...you're right." Margaret, too, traced the blank with her finger. Sure enough, those letters fit perfectly.

"Sometimes this fruit is crushed and added to a stew. The kitchen man—uh, I forgot to ask his name, but he said so."

from Ban

"Oh…"

"Apparently this fruit is only harvested in this region. No wonder we didn't get it!" Grace said happily. Margaret looked down at the puzzle anew.

"Come to think of it—this was inserted by a page that showed this castle." The princess remembered the time she'd started working on it with Veronica and Elizabeth. It seemed not only the name of the lake but also all the other vague hints had something to do with this castle.

"Maybe there are other answers that only people here would know!"

"Yes!" Margaret met Grace's eyes and stood up.

"Hello," Grace called at the kitchen entrance.

"Oh, it's you," a voice replied, and the young blond man came forth.

"I'm sorry about earlier."

"No, I'm the one—whoa!" The young man widened his eyes when he realized that Margaret was standing behind Grace. He hurriedly took a step back and bowed his head.

"P-Princess, what brings you to such a squalid place? …Y-You didn't rattle on me, did you?" The young man glanced at Grace with frightened eyes, but she furiously waved both her hands.

"No, no! Actually, Her Highness has something she would like to ask you."

"Me?"

Margaret smiled at the bewildered young man. "Pleased to

meet you. I'm Margaret Liones. Thank you for always making such delicious food."

"No, that…um…. Excuse me for not being able to serve anything to your liking."

"No, pardon me. I'm sorry I can't eat much. What's your name?"

"I'm Phil."

"Phil. Well, Phil, there's something I'd like to ask you." Margaret handed the puzzle that she held in her left hand over to Phil. "This is something I brought from the capital. I just can't for the life of me fill in spots like this one…or this one. But just now, we figured out 'cirin fruit,' and we thought maybe we should ask someone who is better acquainted with this region…"

"Huh, let me take a quick look." Phil took the sheet from Margaret and for a while compared the hints with the empty places on the puzzle, lowering his fingers from time to time to count letters, until finally, he nodded. "Well, these certainly aren't the kinds of things you would know. Almost all of these blanks are vegetables, fish…anyways, ingredients associated with this area."

"I thought so." Grace was beaming. "I wonder if the person who made this puzzle is from around here. But Ladies Veronica and Elizabeth found it at a bookstore in the capital, didn't they?"

"Yes…"

"The herbs and other leafy vegetables are almost all things we grow in the garden here. Would you like to see?"

At Phil's words, Margaret smiled and replied, "Really? I'd love to."

from Ban

"Right this way." Returning the puzzle to Margaret's hand, Phil invited the two of them into the kitchen. They passed before the sink, opened the wooden door at the far end, and found themselves in the courtyard. Enclosed by the keep, its two towers, and the ramparts that connected them, the courtyard measured about 160 feet on each side. The brick walkway that linked the keep's front entrance and the gate between the two towers cut through the center. Various garden trees were planted on either side of the path.

"Those far rows over there are vegetables, and that area over there is herbs."

Many varieties of flowering plants grew in the plot where Phil pointed, their leaves all subtly different shades of green. There were tall plants, plants that crawled and spread over the ground, plants with tiny flowers.

"..."

"The potted ones over there are mint. This block is sage. That's lemongrass, and this here is what was in that puzzle just now, 'snow on the mountain'..."

Listening to Phil's explanation, Margaret approached the spot and knelt down in the dirt, unconcerned that her hem would get dirty. Just as the name suggested, the new leaves were whitish in color; it looked as if they were dusted with a light layer of snow.

"..."

When the wind blew, it carried the smell of damp earth and the strong aroma of grass with it. Margaret gently felt the grass before her with her fingers, and when she tore one blade, she caught a sweet scent.

"What a nice smell…it somehow makes me nostalgic," she found herself murmuring. Though she could hardly remember it, she had a feeling that long ago, she'd smelled the same aroma here.

Are you ready?

Not yet!

Gilthunder and Griamore and Veronica and herself.

Hadn't the four of them run around this yard and played hide and seek?

Are you ready?

Not yet!

Tears pooled in Margaret's eyes and dripped down to dampen her cheeks.

4

"Wow, it's true, everything is filled in!" Grace clapped her hands together in celebration.

At the workbench in the kitchen, Margaret scribbled with her feather quill, filling in the final empty spaces of the puzzle with the names of ingredients. She gazed at the beautifully completed puzzle with satisfaction. Then, as if an idea had come to her all of a sudden, she looked up at Phil who stood beside her.

"Hey, Phil…is there a meal that uses all of the ingredients in this puzzle?"

"Let's see… I don't think there is just one meal…but together, hmm…" *Ah!* the cook cried out after deliberating for a moment.

from Ban

"Come to think of it, there was that time…"

"That time?" Grace echoed. Phil, who'd dropped his head to mutter to himself, raised his face.

"Um, I think it was four or five years ago—the 'Seven Deadly Sins' came to this castle."

"The Seven Deadly Sins!" cried Grace.

Phil seemed flustered. "Oh, I'm sorry… They're traitors to the royal family now…" He frantically bowed his head as if to end his story.

"It's all right, I want to hear. What happened with the Seven Deadly Sins?" Margaret asked.

"Usually the only people here are the custodians, but when guests visit from the capital, servants are gathered as they are now. At the time, the cook here was my grandfather. The Seven Deadly Sins were staying here for some kind of mission. I was around twelve, and I sometimes came to help him—that day, when I peered into the kitchen…"

Phil went on to say that the person who was cooking wasn't his grandfather, but a hulking man with silver hair and bright red eyes.

"Silver hair, red eyes and—a giant." Margaret remembered. There was such a man amongst the Seven Deadly Sins. "Ban, the Fox's Sin of Greed?"

"Yes, he was called Ban. He said, 'Hey, help me out here'—and I did because I was scared, but when I tried speaking to him, he was actually fairly friendly and fun…"

And also surprisingly good at cooking, Phil added.

"I think they stayed about ten days. Ban would often lose bets with the others, and the loser had to cook, he said. I think nearly all of the ingredients in the puzzle were in the several dishes that he made then…"

"Ah, I'd like to try them."

Grace and Phil leaned forward at Margaret's murmur.

"R-Really?"

"I'll make it! I'll go buy the ingredients tomorrow!" As Phil spoke, he looked like he just remembered something. "Actually, Ban shared a piece of advice back then… When I asked what the secret was to making good food, he said to 'do the opposite of the Chief's cooking.'"

"The Chief's cooking?"

Yes, Phil affirmed.

"Our chief is absolutely horrible at cooking!" Ban had said, laughing. "Do you know what he said when I asked him how he made his food taste so much like garbage?"

"Wh-What?"

"It's what happens if you disregard the diner's feelings and make only what you want to make! So, to make delicious food, you do the opposite, got it?"

"Maybe, unknowingly, I was only making what I wanted to make. I chose my flavors to avoid being ridiculed as a country chef, but

from Ban

I was only pleasing myself... Ah, um, so..." Phil looked at Margaret. "From the beginning, I should have asked you what you wanted to eat, or how you were feeling today."

"Well, really...I'm sorry I made you so self-conscious."

Grace stepped in between Margaret, who frowned apologetically, and Phil, whose face had clouded over considerably. "That's right! It's almost Her Highness' birthday, isn't it? Why don't we make that meal for her birthday dinner?"

Phil's eyes shone. "Wh-What? When is it?!"

"July 7th!"

Phil and Grace eagerly nodded to each other and looked ready to hold hands as well. Margaret beamed at them with gratitude and cast another glance at the puzzle she held in her hands.

So the Seven Deadly Sins had been here. The puzzle had been next to a page that showed this castle and lake, and the hints were names of ingredients that were often used here. And they'd gone into a meal that one of the Sins had made.

It also had our names, father's magical power, and Zaratras, so I thought one of the capital's Holy Knights or a castle retainer had made it...

If it was the work of one of the Seven Deadly Sins, however, the sentence written at the bottom of the puzzle: "The one who solves it all shall kiss the witch and gain an invitation to the banquet"...

Kiss—the witch?

The witch among the Seven Deadly Sins could only be the Boar's Sin of Gluttony, Merlin.

Merlin...M-E-R-L-I-N...

"Oh..." Margaret realized. Right around the middle of the puzzle, if she diagonally followed the "M" that started her own name, it spelled M-E-R-L-I-N.

"......"

Margaret gently pressed her lips over the name.

Then—

"Ah!"

Suddenly, the puzzle began to sparkle. Margaret, and of course Grace and Phil beside her, were stunned. The three of them stared at the shining puzzle.

"Aie!"

A bunch of letters she'd inscribed in the puzzle jumped out, glittering gold. They swirled and danced in the air before finally lining up to form a sentence.

"'GO TO THE BASEMENT'?"

At that moment, beneath their feet—

Thunk... It sounded like something large had moved.

5

When they followed the message and headed to the aged castle's basement, a small room that was being used to store food, they discovered a passage had opened in the stone wall in the back. At the end of the stairs that continued from there was a large secret chamber.

"Wow...amazing..." Phil, who carried a lantern and stepped

in first, blurted out in wonder. The chamber was twenty feet long and wide, and the ceiling stood over ten feet tall. A large window hollowed out in one of the walls was inlaid with vivid stained glass. It seemed strange that a basement room should have a window, but apparently it opened to the island's cliff and must have been invisible from the outside due to some kind of magic. The stained glass was a geometric pattern made up of a combination of several colored glass squares about four inches on each side. The rainbow light that shone through it cast the same design upon the stone floor.

"How beautiful…"

In the center of the room was a wooden table that should have been too large to bring down here. A white earthenware tea set for five was laid upside down on a beautifully textured wooden tray. The chamber hadn't been visited in so long that a layer of dust coated everything, but there were no strange odors.

"This stained glass design…is the same as that puzzle, isn't it?" Grace said while gently touching the glass.

"Ah…you're right." Margaret turned toward the window and held up the puzzle. Sure enough, it was exactly the same.

"The invitation to the banquet—I wonder if it was the right to enter this room?"

"Perhaps the Deadly Sins held banquets here." Margaret smiled.

"That's it! How about we have our banquet here as well?" It was Phil who said this. "A banquet for Her Highness' birthday. Please have your feast here."

The Seven Deadly Sins

"Lovely!" Grace clapped her hands and hopped. "I'll put some fight into cleaning this room! I'll have Erica and Agatha help as well and have this place sparkling!"

Phil and Grace were looking at each other again and nodding.

Seeing the two of them like that, Margaret pulled up the hem of her dress and gave a lady's curtsy.

"Really—thank you. I'll look forward to it."

"No, Your Highness, it's nothing!"

As the two of them gaped in humble surprise, the princess smiled at them with all of her heart.

Chapter Six
The Fate Altered by the Giant

—from Diane

Rain continued to fall.

The weather in Britannia at the beginning of spring was unstable, so rain itself was not rare.

But a rain so violent, and that continued for so long, was very unusual. It had already been several days. The showers became stronger each day and showed no signs of stopping whatsoever.

Yet another day had passed since Diane became confined to that place. For the woman, who was part of the giant clan, it was difficult to find somewhere her large body could escape the rain. After wandering among the mountains, she crouched in the shadow of a huge rock she'd finally found, holding her knees.

"Chief... I wonder how he's doing."

Diane didn't really know what had happened. She'd been summoned by Zaratras, the Captain of the Holy Knights, regarding some kind of grave matter, only to find him stabbed to death. What's more, before she knew it, she found herself surrounded by the kingdom's Holy Knights.

If she and the others tried in earnest, then destroying the capital might have been easy, but they couldn't possibly do that. At that moment, all they could do was split up and run.

We were supposed to rendezvous later, but as for where and how...we didn't decide a thing...

The Seven Deadly Sins

Diane's large frame was easy to spot, and news of her sightings seemed to circulate immediately. How many Holy Knights had she battled until she found that rock? From the information she gathered in those moments, it seemed that Zaratras' younger brother, Dreyfus, and Hendrickson had taken command. Were they the masterminds? She didn't know.

The only thing she did know was that they, the Seven Deadly Sins, had been set up by somebody. As to who—she no longer cared, figuring that it was just the way humans were.

"I don't care anymore..." Her stomach was empty and she was drowsy. She had a feeling that some time long ago, she'd held her knees in the shadow of a boulder, alone like this. As to when, though, she couldn't remember.

The rain continued to hammer down upon the boulder. She could hear the rumbling noise of rushing water from somewhere. She remembered that there was a creek not far from where she sat. It had to be the sound's source.

But—somehow, it's a little strange...

It was too ferocious for a stream, and occasionally she even felt tremors in the earth. Diane reluctantly left the shelter of the boulder for the rain and began walking through the forest.

Oh!

Peering through the shadows, she swallowed her breath. The sheer volume of it was incredible. The muddy flow swallowed up huge boulders, snapped trees at the roots, and rushed downstream in a powerful torrent.

Actually, wasn't there a human village downstream?

from Diane

She'd caught a glimpse of it the day before in passing. If a current of such strength reached that settlement, it would be gone in a moment.

Did everyone escape already?

It's been raining for so many days... They must have run away long ago...

Still—some people might have missed their chance.

Diane shook her head emphatically.

"Nothing to do with me."

All humans were selfish and cunning and only thought about using others. Yes, they were always like that. Always.

"..."

Diane dropped her gaze to the ground.

But maybe, that village—is the one we passed through a few years ago on a mission.

All of the Seven Deadly Sins had stayed in an old castle on a lake farther downstream. But Diane the giant, unable to enter, had slept alone on the bank. At that time, a few mischievous children had come all the way from a nearby village to see the giant. Hiding timidly, but with twinkling eyes, they had peered up at Diane.

"It doesn't matter, really." Diane clenched her teeth.

Then slowly, she knelt and pushed both her palms against the ground.

"Why am I doing this?"

Magical power surged from her body. It was swallowed by the earth. Before long, off in the distance, she heard intense tremors.

The Seven Deadly Sins

1

"See? We're starting to see it," Griamore said, pulling his horse toward the carriage. Elizabeth's head poked out from a window.

"Really? Where?"

"Ellie! Don't stand, it's dangerous!" Veronica's voice came from inside, but Elizabeth wouldn't listen. She leaned out until her shoulders were nearly outside as well.

"You don't need to do that, you'll see it clearly if we go a little further—see?"

The carriage slowly rounded a bend in the mountain road. Before long, a large lake stretched before them.

"Wow!"

"There. You see it, yes? Near the shore on our side, on that island, is the royal villa."

It was just as Griamore said. On the lake's placid, glimmering surface, which reflected the mountains on the opposite shore, floated a small island, upon which stood a cozy little castle.

"That's where sister is!"

"Ellie, it's dangerous so sit! We're almost there!"

Rebuked by Veronica, Elizabeth's face finally withdrew from the window.

"Is it true that I visited once before as a baby?" Just her voice was audible through the window as she spoke to Veronica.

"It seems so. I was still young, too, and don't remember anything," Veronica replied. Hearing that, Griamore called to Gilthunder, who rode a little ahead of him.

from Diane

"Do you remember, Gil? We went there as well, years ago— were we about six?"

"Who knows? Were we?" Gilthunder answered curtly.

"I don't recall much of it either, but I think we played hide and seek in the courtyard. Looking at that castle now, I feel like I'm starting to remember." Griamore narrowed his eyes and urged his horse forward to line up beside Gilthunder. "Hey, are you really not going to stop by the castle? Princess Margaret is there, isn't she?"

"I'm not," Gilthunder said without looking over. "You're more than capable of dropping Veronica and Elizabeth off at the castle on your own."

"Yup, yup. Let's go on ahead. I'm burning to test it." Howzer, who was walking his horse in front of the carriage, loosened his reins slightly to approach them. He was carrying a long spear under his arm. He badly wanted to try out the new weapon he had received from Dreyfus, the Holy Knight Captain.

"You there, keep the chattering in moderation," Holy Knight Nicholas called out from the other side of the two horses pulling the carriage. *Y-Yes,* responded the three apprentices, who were childhood friends, before quickly separating their horses.

Their destination was not the royal family's villa up ahead but a small village farther north.

Werewolves had appeared near the village, which was called Isula, and killed several inhabitants. The report had reached the capital only recently.

It was decided that Nicholas would investigate the state of

affairs, and the apprentices were ordered to accompany him. Hearing that Isula was in the same direction as the royal villa, Veronica demanded that she be brought along and ended up following in a carriage.

Before long, the party saw a forked road ahead of them. The path on the left swerved from the mountains and headed down toward the lake. The path on the right continued on, toward the village of Isula.

"Well then, I'll escort Princesses Veronica and Elizabeth to the villa." Griamore stopped his horse and raised a hand toward Nicholas and the others as the carriage turned its nose to the left and began to clatter down the hill.

"Ah, send Princess Margaret my best regards. Take care."

"Yes, sir. After I say hello, I'll catch up to you!"

Watching Griamore follow after the carriage, Gilthunder halted his horse for just a moment.

Past the brush-laden, untamed hills was the lake's sparkling surface. The bright summer sun shone high in the heavens. From where Gilthunder stood, the island and castle floating on the shining mirror of a lake appeared as silhouettes, with only the shapes of the two towers and the keep's roof in distinct relief. Neither the windows nor the yard was visible.

Margaret was there.

Gilthunder gazed at the silhouette wistfully. Even those few seconds of reflection were interrupted by the ringing caw of a raven from above. Gilthunder quietly spurred his horse and caught up with Howzer and the others.

from Diane

2

"Hmm...so this is the first time a werewolf has attacked humans?" Nicholas stooped uncomfortably to ask the elderly man, who stood only half as tall as the Holy Knight.

"That is so. Originally, up until about three years ago, this area wasn't even connected to the mountains where the werewolves live. Yes, that was right after the news spread of the Seven Deadly Sins' mutiny." The elderly man, who was the village mayor, stretched up to point at the distant mountains. "That year, there were torrential rains in these parts, and this village was almost swallowed by the rising stream. At the last moment, however, the flow shifted."

"The flow shifted?"

"Indeed. West of the village, you saw a large difference in elevation, did you not? Now it is a garden, but the stream flowed there before. A mountain upstream collapsed, and the terrain transformed—"

The village of Isula was a small settlement of houses dotting a narrow bit of flat land between the mountains. The villagers grew vegetables in tiny plots and kept goats and sheep in the hills. It seemed there were also people who hunted.

"I see. So the stream's course twisted further away. You narrowly escaped death."

"But with that mountain collapsing, a previously impassable cliff was leveled, and the wolves began to come down from the Black Fog Mountains on the other side. It seems the wolf-men's territory was also up there… Last month several were killed."

"I see—how many werewolves?"

"There were two then, and a hunter felled one of them. As for how many more…"

"It doesn't matter!" Howzer blurted out impatiently. "Who cares how many, let's just wipe them out!"

"You know we can't do that." Nicholas smiled bitterly. "Anyways, we'll scout it out before Griamore returns."

"Yes, sir," Gilthunder nodded. *Thank you kindly,* the village mayor lowered his head.

"But how odd—wolf-men… Their numbers are already very few," Nicholas remarked as he trod the mountain path that continued from Isula toward the Black Fog Mountains.

"I hear they're quite strong," Howzer said.

"Only on nights when the moon is full or nearly full. During the day, not so much. To begin with, as the name 'wolf-man' suggests, only some males are able to assume a perfectly human form, or so I've been told. Well, the females rarely leave their territory, so we don't actually know…"

"In that case, let's just attack them during the day."

"In theory this is true. However, if it's a matter of their territory shifting due to a change in terrain, there might a way of settling this peacefully by addressing that issue."

"Seriously? How boring!" Howzer hoisted his spear.

"Now, don't say that. It's always best not to get into a fight," Nicholas, who was a large but kind man, chided with a smile.

from Diane

Listening to their conversation, Gilthunder alone walked in silence. These parts were cool even in the summer, and at such a high elevation, they didn't see many large trees even deep into the mountains. Instead, large boulders and naked cliffs continued endlessly, and a white haze that was neither cloud nor fog hung just above them, reducing visibility. The ground was so thoroughly sodden that tiny rivulets had formed in several places.

"Hmmm—this area?" Nicholas, who led the group, halted. "It seems this is where we enter their territory. Sure enough, the paths around here look new—now, what to do."

"I'll go and look a little further," Gilthunder said and began to march on without waiting for Nicholas' reply.

"Hey, be careful. Don't venture too far."

"I'll go too!"

Gilthunder heard Howzer but hurried on without waiting.

He wanted to be alone.

He'd come so close to Margaret and still couldn't meet her. When he first received his mission, his heart thrilled to the idea of approaching her at least, but now, after passing that place by, his heart only ached.

I wanted to come. I shouldn't have come.

Tossed about by those two sentiments, Gilthunder just clenched his teeth and proceeded along the mountain path.

3

"It really is pretty, dear sister!" Elizabeth happily spread out the hem of her dress with both hands. As she did, the light filtering through the stained glass made her white dress look like a beautiful piece of rainbow-colored cloth.

They were at the north villa, in the basement chamber that Margaret had found.

"To think that such a secret was hidden in this puzzle... I wonder who made it." Veronica, too, spoke with admiration as she held the puzzle up to the stained glass.

Margaret smiled but didn't reveal that the answer to her sister's question was the Seven Deadly Sins. Veronica had always abhorred the Sins as strange, evil people, and since Zaratras' death, she disliked hearing even their names.

"Your Highnesses, the meal is ready for you in the dining room," Grace, the maid, came to call them.

"I want to eat here—you held big sister's birthday celebration in this room, didn't you?" Elizabeth said, a little dissatisfied.

"Perhaps tomorrow we can have them bring it down here," Margaret suggested with a chuckle before gently pressing on Elizabeth's shoulder. "Now, go on up. You too, Veronica."

"Okay!" the younger sisters answered brightly and followed after Grace to exit the chamber.

After watching the two of them leave, Margaret stood before the stained glass again and looked up at the beautiful geometric pattern. Every time she came here, her heart felt just a little lighter. Was it because memories from a distant day seemed to envelope her?

"Hmm, I see." A woman's voice suddenly spoke right beside

from Diane

Margaret and made her jump away.

"Vivian!"

It was she who stood there. Vivian wasn't wearing a mask, but in her right hand, she held the staff shaped like a monster's hand.

"'The one who solves it all shall kiss the witch and gain an invitation to the banquet'..." Vivian grabbed the puzzle from the tabletop and, like Veronica, held it up against the stained glass. "I know this handwriting. It belongs to one of the Seven Deadly Sins, the Goat's Sin of Lust, Gowther. 'Kiss the witch'—huh."

"Vivian...please give it back," Margaret pleaded. Vivian, however, merely narrowed her eyes and continued to gaze at the puzzle.

"So you kissed that woman's name in this puzzle, and found this chamber."

"Yes..."

"But that doesn't mean you've solved this puzzle."

"What?"

Vivian laughed triumphantly. "'An invitation to the banquet'— this room? You think?" Holding the puzzle up to the stained glass once more, she slowly recited some kind of spell. Then, all of the letters written in the puzzle sprang up in the stained glass as well. "Stained glass with the same pattern as the puzzle... Naturally, there'd be another twist," she muttered and stepped up to the wall.

Tracing her finger over the floating letters spelling MERLIN, Vivian hesitated for a few seconds before knitting her brow and whirling around to face Margaret.

"Nope! Your Highness, you do it."

"Do...what?"

"It's obvious! 'Kiss the witch.'"

Margaret squeezed the hem of her dress but saw fit to do as Vivian said. Placing one hand on the stained glass, she softly pressed her lips against the "R" of MERLIN.

Then…

"Ahh!" Just like with the puzzle, a bunch of letters inscribed in the stained glass sparkled and flickered and leapt out into the air to form a sentence.

But these letters were no longer from the alphabet, somehow having turned into runes used by magicians. Margaret couldn't decipher it.

The moment Vivian saw the line, her face changed color. "That woman… So she was hiding it in such a place!"

"Vivian!" Margaret cried out. She had a bad feeling.

But not sparing the princess another glance, the witch vanished with a single wave of her staff.

4

The fog steadily grew thicker as Gilthunder walked the narrow path. Until moments earlier, there were still signs of Howzer behind him, but not anymore. Perhaps he'd taken a wrong path somewhere.

Had he? Or had Howzer? Either way, Gilthunder needed to turn back. No matter how lengthy a summer day, these were the mountains. It was already growing dark.

Still, he pressed on.

from Diane

He began not to care where he was going, or why. He just wanted to disappear into the fog. As the thought crossed his mind—

Rustle, came a sound from up ahead. Gilthunder's hand shot to his sword's hilt.

"Who goes there?!"

"Wait!" bade a mild voice.

She appeared in the fog—a young woman, slightly older than Gilthunder. She had a slender build and wore hunting garments. Her silver hair was tied up behind her head.

"I'm Blanca. I'm a hunter from the village at the northern foot of the mountains. I strayed too far and lost my way."

"This path leads to the village of Isula, in the hinterlands of Liones." Gilthunder squinted and looked over the women's appearance. There was nothing particularly suspicious about her.

"I see. So I must have passed over the ridge and come out on the other side."

"If you go straight down this path, I think you'll find my group. Please join with them and leave the mountains. I'm sure it's past sunset now."

"What are you going to do?" Blanca asked, tilting her head.

"I'm...going a little further."

"I heard werewolves prowl past here. It's dangerous."

"I know." He did. "It's dangerous—that's why I'm going."

"I see—so..." Blanca's voice grew quiet. "You're also—out to slay wolves."

Something about her tone made Gilthunder shudder, and he

did a double take. "I…"

Blanca's blue-gray eyes flashed in the fog. Gazing into Gilthunder's, she suddenly took a deep breath.

Ooooo…

Howzer stopped in his tracks when he heard a wolf's howl in the distance. Realizing that he'd lost sight of Gilthunder somewhere along the way, he was retracing his path.

He gripped his spear and listened. The howling echoed amidst the rocks and fog, and he couldn't pinpoint its source.

"Gil!" The fog swallowed up his call. He couldn't tell how far it traveled. "Gilthunder! Hey!"

Did the wolf's howl reach Nicholas as well? Was he heading this way?

In any case, clearing away the fog seemed like a good idea. Just when Howzer started to think his wind magic might be up to the task—

"……"

A human shadow swayed onto a boulder just to his right.

"Gil!" It was Gilthunder. Relieved, Howzer smiled at his friend. "Hey, did you hear the howling just now? I wonder which way it came from. Did you see a wolf?"

"…"

"Anyways, let's return to Nicholas. Or do you want to look for the wolf together?" proposed Howzer, laughing.

It was at that moment.

Gilthunder suddenly raised his blade and leapt from the

from Diane

boulder.

"Whoa!"

Howzer jumped back immediately, but Gilthunder struck again the moment he landed. Howzer used the shaft of his spear to block the sideways swipe just in time.

"What the heck?!"

"Dead…"

"What?"

"You're dead."

Gilthunder's eyes were hollow, and they didn't settle on anything. Seeing this, Howzer finally realized that Gilthunder wasn't in his right mind.

"H-Hey, Gil! Wake up!"

"I'll avenge them—you're dead! You humans are all dead!"

"Gil!" At close quarters, Howzer would be at a disadvantage with his spear. Frantically dodging Gilthunder's blade, which swung again and again, or parrying it with his own weapon, Howzer shouted, "Gil! What are you doing?!"

The words fell on deaf ears.

Gilthunder's sword closed in, giving Howzer no time to think.

Eh, I don't have a choice!

Shoving Gilthunder away forcefully, Howzer held his spear aslant. Fortunately, his friend was weaker than usual, robbed of his mind. It seemed he couldn't even use his magical powers.

"This would've been difficult a little while ago, but with Lord Dreyfus' spear…"

I'll blast him away without hurting him, and then…

from Diane

Howzer imagined the wind blowing. He wanted to seal Gilthunder's movements, and also signal Nicholas if possible.

With his current skills—with this spear, perhaps he could pull it off.

"Here goes, Gilthunder! Wall Shock!"

A swirling mass of wind blasted Gilthunder away. Then from beneath his floating body struck a tornado.

"Rising Tornado!!"

"Aaahhhh!"

Gilthunder's scream echoed, and the fog scattered.

5

"I see…so this is Merlin's magic square."

Hendrickson looked around with his arms crossed. He was deep under the royal family's villa, in a different spot from the chamber that Margaret and the others had found. That room was right beneath the keep, but this place seemed to be positioned under the tower. The nearly perpendicular walls and floors carved into the natural cliff were covered with complex patterns.

"With this," flared Vivian, "even considerably difficult fusions will be feasible—yes, for instance, beasts and plants, or even fish can be combined."

Hmm, Hendrickson pondered. "You said the other day: crossing strong animals helter-skelter only unbalances them because their powers conflict."

"Yes. And I don't think using a magic square would change

that."

"Right, no matter how strong the synthesis, it might be pointless if it has the intellect of a beast."

"I'm sure that's true..." Vivian looked up, her face pale. "Um—you cannot be planning on using humans?"

"Hah..." Barely listening to Vivian, Hendrickson murmured with a hand on his chin, "What's amplified through a demon's blood are emotions that the subject already felt. And not simple ones like anger or fear, but rather, inner conflicts like envy, resentment, and rancor—they tend to create the best responses."

Vivian quaked at his flat voice. What was it that allowed him to be so cold-hearted?

Restoring the demon clan so that chaos would engulf the world again. There, only the truly strong would reign as beacons of light and guide people. Overturning a world filled with a deceptive, false peace, so that the insulted might reclaim their pride.

Was the man aspiring to become a demon god for the sake of that ideal?

"Yes...it's worth a try. Before we turn to humans."

"Hendrickson..."

The man chuckled at Vivian, who was trembling. "Don't worry, I won't use humans yet. Apparently, there are fitting subjects not far from here."

Chapter Seven
The Courage Charm and Their Vows
—from Meliodas

Gilthunder ran over the stone-paved path, bathed in the morning light. Surely at that hour, Meliodas was warming up in front of the lodging house. It was his daily routine.

Ah, there he was. The small form atop the stone bridge was that of the Seven Deadly Sins' leader.

"Sir Meliodas!"

Meliodas turned around at the sound of Gilthunder's voice and flashed his usual smile—not knowing anything.

"Hey, Gil boy. Today's the kingdom's anniversary festival!"

The yearly commemoration...

The castle town would soon be filled with dressed-up people if this were like any other year.

"Tell your father that I challenge him to a drinking con—"

"Run away!!" Gilthunder shouted, his breath ragged. Tears spilled from his eyes.

"Run...what is this, all of a sudden?" Meliodas questioned with a blank stare.

"Something horrible is going to happen to you and the others... Nkk."

"Why don't you explain it to me in detail?"

"That's...not possible!! If it gets out that I talked about it..." Clutching Meliodas, Gilthunder groaned. He had to tell, yet couldn't say anything. He didn't know how to save both the Seven Deadly Sins and Margaret, whom he loved. "What do I do...what can I—"

"Calm down!"

Meliodas delivered a chop to the crown of Gilthunder's head. It was in jest but hurt considerably, and Gilthunder cradled his poor skull.

"I don't know what happened, but you just think about what you need to do," Meliodas said, staring Gilthunder straight in the eye. "What do you need to do?"

Meliodas was always right. He always showed the way.

Gilthunder sniffled and, wiping his tears with the back of his hand, answered, "I have to...protect Margaret."

Yes. He was her knight. He had to protect her. That was his number-one duty.

"All right, good!" Meliodas smiled. He must have guessed from Gilthunder's demeanor that this was nothing trivial, but still he remained calm.

"B-But I'm not sure I can, alone..."

Gilthunder had always been protected, if not by this man, then by his father Zaratras, or his uncle Dreyfus, or by Hendrickson. He also had his friends, Howzer and Griamore. When he was in trouble, he had many people to talk to...

But. He was going to lose all of that. From now on he couldn't depend on anybody.

"Then I'll teach you a charm." Although Meliodas knew nothing yet, he laughed as though he did. "Recite it when you're down and out but can't depend on anybody."

"A...charm?"

Meliodas stared into Gilthunder's eyes. "Yes. It goes, 'I'm stronger than any of the Seven Deadly Sins'!!"

"I-I'm stronger than any of the Seven Deadly Sins?"

There, Meliodas nodded and lightly thumped his fist against Gilthunder's chest. "Well? You feel braver, don't you? If you're stronger than any of us, there's nothing to be afraid of, eh?"

With that, he gathered Gilthunder into his arms. Meliodas' small but powerful hands ruffled Gilthunder's red hair.

"Don't worry, Gil boy. When you're in a pinch, I'll always help you."

"Meliodas!!"

Gilthunder clung to him and began to cry again. Meliodas just continued to embrace the sobbing boy, who still wasn't explaining a thing.

1

"Hey, hey, Gilthunder, get it together!"

Gilthunder awoke as someone patted his cheek.

"Where am I..."

"Isula."

Howzer and Griamore were hovering over him. Gilthunder sat up in a panic. He was lying on a plain bed in someone's home.

"Where am—what happened to me?"

Howzer laughed. "So you don't remember anything? All right,

fine. You were possessed by a wolf."

Hearing those words, Gilthunder remembered. No, perhaps it would be more accurate to say that he understood. "Blanca—where's Blanca?!"

"Blanca? You mean that wolf? It's gone now," Nicholas said, opening the door and coming in.

"Gone?"

"We caught it while you were out. That was the werewolf clan's magical Howling—they say it can manipulate beasts, but I didn't know that humans are also susceptible. The moon is far from full, so I'd let down my guard."

"If you captured her, how's she gone? Did you kill her?"

"No. Last night, Holy Knight Captain Hendrickson arrived with a magician in tow. They took it away immediately with a teleportation spell. They're going to interrogate it back at the capital. Female werewolves are rare, so no wonder Lord Hendrickson is interested."

"—…!!"

Pushing Howzer and the others out of the way, Gilthunder jumped out of bed. He rushed over to the door and sprang into the open air.

It was bright outside. It seemed it was almost noon.

Gilthunder scanned the area. Of course, there was already no sign of Hendrickson.

However.

"What…"

Gilthunder widened his eyes.

from Meliodas

The village was devastated. The crops in the outlying fields were violently uprooted, and the roofs and walls of several houses were damaged.

"This too…is her doing?"

"By her, you mean the wolf," Howzer responded to Gilthunder's question and shrugged. It seemed they hadn't seen her take human form.

"To be precise, it was the beasts manipulated by that thing," Griamore said. "A little after you went scouting, a huge bear attacked all of a sudden. Also a host of deer, wild rabbits, mice, and so on—the village was in an uproar when I arrived." He sighed before continuing, "Even rabbits and mice are a handful if there are enough of them. The larger beasts like the bear and the deer, we were able to take down immediately. The mice, though, snuck into houses and bit children, while the rabbits dug holes and undermined pillars…"

Apparently, they had evacuated the elderly and children before exterminating the small animals painstakingly with the help of the local adults.

"Tsk, not exactly the job of a Holy Knight."

Griamore's weary face had Howzer rolling on the ground laughing.

Gilthunder looked up at the cloudy sky and bit his lip.

When Blanca had put him under a spell, Gilthunder had seen her mind.

She was the last survivor of the werewolf clan that had lived in the heart of the mountains.

The Seven Deadly Sins

Humans were encroaching on their territory since the shift in terrain and overhunting. With the game growing scarce, the were-wolves, and their thralls the sword wolves, had no choice but to descend into civilized lands, but that angered the humans in turn. An extensive wolf hunt was conducted, and the sword wolf pack was annihilated. Their flayed skins and extracted fangs were sold to the markets.

You shan't be forgiven.

Gilthunder could still feel Blanca's howl in his ears.

"Anyways, the problem has been resolved. Let's return to the capital," Nicholas said, patting Gilthunder on the shoulder.

2

The strange spell that Vivian was chanting echoed through the underground cavern.

Synchronized with her intonation, the complex magic square drawn on the walls and floor flickered.

Crouched on the floor at the center was a large shadow. Its original shape and color was impossible to discern with the ceiling and wall lights glinting on its back.

"It's good—it's perfect, Hendrickson," Vivian exulted. Hendrickson nodded and approached the shadow.

"Do you want power?" he whispered to it. "Do you hate the humans who robbed you of your friends, your home? Do you seek magical power unbound by the phases of the moon?"

"I do…"

from Meliodas

"I'll make you stronger than the legendary Seven Deadly Sins."

"Seven...Deadly Sins," the shadow moaned.

Hendrickson nodded and held up a tiny needle in his right hand.

The needle—was plunged into the shadow's body.

"Aa...aaaah!" With a ringing cry of agony, the shadow writhed. It rose up, swelling.

"Is it...not working?" asked Vivian. But—the thing didn't burst open.

"We're good."

Gaaaah, the monster's howl shook the room.

"Eek!" Vivian quickly tried to stop its movements with a spell. However, she was a moment too late. The monster's body swung around and sent her flying. Before she could even scream, she struck the wall and passed out.

"I see... Nice. Quite the success." Hendrickson snickered. "Now—shall we put it to the test?"

3

"Ugh, is this it?" Howzer muttered and yawned atop his horse. "Why couldn't we have gone there as well?" His finger pointed at the small island on the lake.

They were at the fork in the mountain road where they'd split up with Veronica and the others. Originally, they were supposed to join back up with the princesses on their way home, but having completed their mission sooner than expected, Griamore had gone to ask what they were to do.

"Not visiting in droves is also Princess Margaret's wish. Stop griping and just wait a bit," Nicholas said, chuckling. Right at that moment—

Bom, a jolt seemed to push up the earth.

"Wha?!"

"Ah, the island!" Howzer pointed at the lake.

"____!!"

Half of the tiny island where the royal villa stood suddenly burst and threatened to crumble off.

Without uttering a word, Gilthunder spurred his horse and sped down the road toward the lake at a full gallop.

Fortunately, the castle was on the island's northern side, which was still unharmed. Griamore was there, so things had to be under control.

"Wait, Gil! We'll go too!"

Gilthunder heard Howzer's voice, followed by hoofbeats, but hadn't the time to look back.

In the distance—a wolf howled.

The same voice as before shook Gilthunder's mind.

Dead.

Hate.

Vengeance.

You're dead.

He tightened the reins right away. His horse reared up. Out of the corner of his eye he glimpsed someone else's mount doing the same.

Hadn't Gilthunder been thrown off his horse and flung to the ground? But there was no pain, or any other sensation.

When he lifted his head, he saw that Howzer was on his feet aiming his spear skyward. Who was he fighting?

Gilthunder's vision misted over and he couldn't see very well.

Then, he saw blood. Somebody had fallen.

A large black shadow swooped down from the heavens.

He couldn't hear anything. There was—no sound.

Everything looked gray.

The claws of a huge bird. Bright white wings spread.

Dead.

A snake made of water soared up. Nicholas' spell? Where was he?

The wind raged. Howzer. But who? Who was there?

His own hand had at some point found his sword. Blue-white lightning gathered at its tip.

Dead.

Howzer turned around, but their eyes didn't meet. Why was he thrusting his spear at Gilthunder?

Dead.

Whose voice was that? Howzer? Nicholas? Or…

Dead.

It was—his own. The voice had issued from Gilthunder's own lips.

Lightning tore through the air. At the same time, Howzer's tornado was closing in.

Gilthunder swung his sword. Several thunderbolts shot into the ground, blasting away nearby trees.

Even then—there was no sound at all. He couldn't smell anything, either.

It didn't feel real. It was like watching a chain of events unfolding well away.

You're dead.

Dimly, in the corner of his mind, Gilthunder thought that they were being made to kill each other.

It was Blanca's power.

From the moment they heard the howling, their bodies had been taken over.

Somebody was laughing, far up in the sky. Gilthunder craned his neck sluggishly.

It was a beautiful creature.

A huge wolf's head with dark pupils and a bright red mouth.

A woman's ample-breasted torso, covered in fur that glinted silver. Yet both her arms were snow-white wings. Her rear limbs, too, were those of a raptor.

Instead of a bird's tail feathers was the long tail of a wolf.

The word "chimera" flitted across Gilthunder's mind.

The monster swooped down and was tearing something apart with its mouth. Blood sprayed.

He realized somebody had been killed.

It would be his turn next—for sure.

from Meliodas

But it couldn't be helped, could it? Blanca's sorrow and wrath were natural. Robbed of her friends, her lover, she was alone. She'd been living peacefully in the mountains but had lost everything.

He was—tired. Of bearing it alone.

Someone like him ought to just fade away, no doubt.

He wanted to relax. Soon. He'd give up on everything.

Joyous laughter filled his ears.

"Certainly powerful—power! Stronger than the Seven Deadly Sins of legend!"

Blanca's voice? Perhaps it was somebody else's.

Yet—those words pierced the light in Gilthunder's chest that was flickering out.

"Stronger—than the Seven Deadly Sins?"

I'll teach you a charm, he heard Meliodas' words from back then. *Recite it when you're down and out but can't depend on anybody—"I'm stronger than any of the Seven Deadly Sins"!*

They alone—provided uncommon support to Gilthunder.

"Stronger—than the Seven Deadly Sins?"

Impossible.

You just think about what you need to do.

Gilthunder was remembering now. One thing after another.

The Seven Deadly Sins

What do you need to do?

What he needed to do. There was—only one thing.

I have to…protect Margaret.

"Margaret!" shouted Gilthunder. Suddenly color returned to the world.

Somehow he'd ended up on all fours. Using his sword like a cane, he got to his feet.

"S-Sir Nicholas…"

It was Nicholas who was lying drenched in blood. A Holy Knight didn't go down so easily. He must have fallen protecting the apprentices.

A silver wolf with huge wings crouched over his body.

"Blanca! Enough!" Gilthunder screamed and unleashed a thunderbolt at the same time. The monster spread both its wings and flew aside, then rose swiftly up into the air.

"Urk…"

Gilthunder heard a moan right beside him. Keeping his eyes on the sky, he focused on the presence. Howzer, it seemed.

"Howzer! Are you okay? Stay with me!"

"Urgh…"

Confirming that his comrade had managed to sit up, Gilthunder arced a thunderbolt into the sky. Blanca, who was circling above them, easily dodged the attack.

She flashed a grin. If she used her magical Howling again, all would be lost, but they couldn't fight if they covered their ears.

Right—

from Meliodas

Gilthunder gathered lightning at the tip of his sword. Again he fired at the sky.

"You fool! You won't hit me!" Blanca mocked and sucked in her breath again. The blast shot past her and tore through the air with an intense crackling noise. Altering its trajectory according to the movements of the tip of Gilthunder's sword, the bolt struck a bush a little distance away.

"——!!"

Gilthunder's eardrums rang from the explosion. Across from him, Howzer was opening and closing his mouth, but there was no telling what he was saying. Even Blanca's howl wouldn't be audible for a little while. Howzer blinked in surprise, realizing Gilthunder's plan. Their eyes met and they nodded.

Let's go!

Reading each other's lips, they boosted their magical powers.

Rising Tornado!

Purge of the Thunder Emperor!

An enormous tornado that seemed to swallow everything absorbed Gilthunder's lightning and quickly rose up.

Combo! Dragon Castle!

A pitch-black thundercloud swirled, and blue-white lightning shot between the tornado and the sky. A roaring sound broke through the ringing in Gilthunder's ears as the winged wolf spiraled and vanished into the maelstrom.

"D-Did we do it?" Howzer's faint cry reached Gilthunder's gradually recovering ears. The tornado dissipated, but there was no sign of Blanca. Perhaps she had been torn apart and scattered.

"No—there!" yelled Gilthunder.

With tattered wings, she had broken out of the tornado. With her last strength, she flew toward the lake.

"Holy! Margaret and the others!"

Two boats floated on the lake's surface. They must have escaped the crumbling island. They seemed to be headed for the far shore.

"Howzer!"

"Crap!" Howzer scraped together his remaining magic to form another tornado. "Gil! You go!"

The tornado enveloped Gilthunder and threw him up into the air. Clearing the brush-covered hills in one leap, he brandished his blade.

Blanca dived, bringing in her wings. Several people were on the boat down below.

I won't make it in time!

A film of light spread out around the boat. It was Griamore's power, Wall.

Blanca was sent hurtling out of her nosedive. Feathers fluttered from her silver wings. She righted herself unsteadily, spreading her wings to hover in the air.

She was trying to howl again!

But at that moment, some sort of spell went off from the opposite shore. Blanca stiffened as if she had been bound.

Now!

Pointing his thunder-infused sword straight downward, Gilthunder plummeted upon her from above. His heated blade penetrated flesh.

A scorched scent, and a long wail.

Entangled with a winged wolf, Gilthunder fell. He smacked into the surface of the lake with intense force, and at last, he lost consciousness.

4

"Gilthunder! Stay with me!" Patted again on the cheek, Gilthunder opened his eyes.

Griamore, Veronica, Elizabeth. Howzer was there too. And behind them, he could see a bashful Margaret.

When he sat up, he was on a beach, probably on the opposite shore.

The two boats had been pulled aground, and a little ways away, several young men and women that he didn't recognize stood in a cluster. They had to be the villa's servants.

Gilthunder, who was not only soaking wet but covered in sand, gave a large sneeze before asking Griamore, "What happened to Blanca...I mean, that chimera? And what was that magic coming from here?" Gilthunder scanned the area; he thought he'd caught a glimpse of a young man earlier, but there was no one like that now.

"I saw him, I think," Griamore said uncertainly. "That was probably...the captain of the Dawn Roar, an order of Holy Knights just assembled by His Majesty, and operating under his

from Meliodas

direct control. If I'm not mistaken, his name is Slader."

"Slader, huh? I suppose father got worried and sent him to check on us."

At Veronica's words, Griamore nodded. "I'm sure that's it. Perhaps he saw something with his Vision."

Gilthunder gazed once again at the old castle and the island. Half of the outcropping had burst and crumbled away. As for the castle, the keep was unharmed, but the two towers tilted dangerously, and a section of the ramparts had cracked and collapsed.

"…"

Gilthunder got up shakily and strode to meet the shoreline.

Silver feathers washed up at his feet.

"Blanca…" Her proud wolf's body had sunk into the lake, probably never to surface again.

I'm—tired. Of bearing it alone.

The sentiment that had dominated his mind earlier—wasn't it Blanca's as well?

Someone like me ought to just fade away, no doubt.

I want to relax. Soon. I'll give up on everything.

I know how you feel—Blanca, Gilthunder whispered in his heart. *I thought so, too…maybe this whole time.*

In truth, perhaps she was an opponent he wasn't supposed to fight.

Even so. Even so.

The Seven Deadly Sins

What do you need to do?

What he needed to do. There was—only one thing.

I have to…protect Margaret.

Gilthunder slowly turned around.

Elizabeth and the others were watching him curiously, while Margaret stood still beside them.

For just a moment, their gazes intersected, but before long she looked down. Gilthunder, too, looked away, toward the ruined old castle.

Recite it when you're down and out but can't depend on anybody—"I'm stronger than any of the Seven Deadly Sins."

Stronger than any of the Seven Deadly Sins.

It probably didn't just mean magical and martial power.

It was said that the seven had committed "sins" worthy of a thousand deaths—but overcoming that, they tried to protect others.

That's their strength.

Surely, he needed to acquire it as well.

No matter whom he hurt.

Even if it meant wronging those like Blanca who suffered as he did.

Isn't that so, Meliodas? Gilthunder whispered in his heart again.

5

"How could you do such a horrible thing! Gil almost died!"

from Meliodas

Meanwhile—atop a hill that overlooked the lake, Vivian was lashing out at Hendrickson. "You promised that no matter what happens, you will at least spare Gil!"

"I know. Don't get so angry. It was just a little mishap," Hendrickson said like it was nothing and cupped his chin. "I guess in the end, the core has to be a human—and an ordinary one would be of no use. Right, it must be on the level of a Holy Knight—"

"Hey, Hendrickson, are you listening?"

Ignoring Vivian's protests, Hendrickson sunk into his own thoughts. "Perhaps—yes, the fairy corpse I acquired recently... Or does it have other uses..."

A strong wind blew, stirring up the rich smell of water and earth. For just a moment, the scent reminded the terrible Holy Knight Captain of his home deep in the forest where he'd spent his earliest days. Quickly, however, it was painted over by darkness.

"Let's go, Vivian."

"Really, you handle your people so roughly."

With a wave of Vivian's staff, the two of them disappeared in a blink.

On the lake, the wakes of two boats returning to the island were a pale glimmer.

"So...this is the real secret of that puzzle." Margaret swallowed, rooted to the spot.

The chimera had destroyed a cliff on the island, exposing the room Vivian and Hendrickson had used for their experiment. What surprised Margaret and the others, however, wasn't the spent magic square. Past it, beyond the demolished wall, was yet another large underground space.

"Wow, wow, wow-w-w!"

Elizabeth dashed into it.

"Watch out, Ellie!" warned Veronica, but Elizabeth only spread both her arms and spun around.

"It's okay, big sister! Look, it's so pretty!"

Greenery was sprouting in the place as the sun streamed in through sundered rock.

"What the... Hey, hey."

Howzer's and Gilthunder's eyes were round, too.

Grass spread over the ground like a lawn, while five large trees stretched up curling out boughs. The trunks rose to the ceiling and the branches filled the cavern; in seconds, thick leaves grew on them, and buds blossomed into flowers of various colors and shapes.

"How...incredible." Grace, Phil, and all the other servants

stared open-mouthed at the miracle unfurling before them.

Before long, the flowers fell from the branches, and swelling fruits took their place, each again unique in shape.

"Hey, look! It became a fish!"

Sure enough, hanging from a branch of the endmost tree where Howzer pointed was a blue fruit that looked like nothing but a fish.

"This over here—a peach? Wait, it has the face of a pig!"

"The one on this branch, what is it? A potato? Potatoes grow on trees?"

"Of course not, Ellie! But...this..."

Veronica, Griamore, and everyone else circled around and around the five trees to marvel at the bizarre fruit that ripened on each bough.

Howzer boldly plucked off a large green fruit. When he placed it on the ground and sliced it with his sword, thick nectar oozed out of it.

"It smells kind of like soup..."

"May I?" Phil rushed over, brought his face close to it, and sniffed. Then he scooped up the nectar with his finger and tasted it.

"Ah, be careful, Phil," Margaret called out, but Phil only shook his head in amazement.

"No, this...is regular soup. Except it's cool..."

"Seriously?" Howzer scooped up the overflowing juice too. "Gah, it is! Tastes like chicken soup!"

"This fruit has rabbit stew in it." Griamore had cut open a

Epilogue

different one on the other side.

"The fish fruit really does smell like fish, doesn't it? If you fried it, I think you could eat it like a normal fish…" Grace was picking and smelling all kinds of fruit as well, together with Erica.

"If we have these trees, we won't have to worry about food for a while…" Phil sounded almost appalled.

"The Witch's Banquet," Margaret murmured. "Lady Merlin created this…"

"Come to think of it," Gilthunder said, "when my father was still with us, he consulted with her about supplies in case we were besieged or a war dragged on…"

Without stepping closer, the two of them stared at each other—and smiled.

It wasn't as if anything had changed. Margaret was still hounded by Vivian's chimera, and Gilthunder was still under the witch's watchful gaze.

But—we're not alone. Margaret glanced around at the others as they frolicked and laughed.

Although she and Gilthunder couldn't confide in anyone, their family and friends were still with them.

And more than anything—someday, surely, the Seven Deadly Sins would return.

The miracle orchard reminded Margaret of that promise.

They would wait for that day. Without giving up, without losing hope, with smiles on their faces.

The Seven Deadly Sins

Someday, the royal capital would surely be rid of its darkness.

Listening to the jubilant voices of her little sisters as they laughed, Margaret placed her hand on her chest and exhaled.

ABOUT THE AUTHORS

Shuka Matsuda briefly worked in design at an ad firm before turning to what she was meant to do. A writing role for the videogame franchise *Far East of Eden* marked her debut as a storyteller. These days she is known for her children's books and YA novels.

Comics artist Nakaba Suzuki made his debut in 1996 with the fantasy-themed *SAVAGE*. His magnum opus *The Seven Deadly Sins* is a winner of the Kodansha Manga Award.

THE SEVEN DEADLY SINS

THE SEVEN DEADLY SINS
Nakaba Suzuki Presents
THE SEVEN DEADLY SINS
1
Nakaba Suzuki Presents
KC
KODANSHA COMICS

ATTACK ON TITAN

ATTACK ON TITAN:
BEFORE THE FALL

The first of the franchise's light novels, this prequel of prequels details the origins of the devices that humanity developed to take on the mysterious Titans.

ATTACK ON TITAN:
KUKLO UNBOUND

Swallowed and regurgitated as an infant by a Titan, an orphan seeks to find and prove himself in this official prequel novel to the smash hit comics series.

ATTACK ON TITAN:
LOST GIRLS

LOST GIRLS tells of the times and spaces in between the plot points, through the eyes and ears of the saga's toughest—but more taciturn—heroines.

LEARN MORE AT

IN NOVEL FORM!

ATTACK ON TITAN: THE HARSH MISTRESS OF THE CITY Part 1

A stand-alone side story, *Harsh Mistress* tells of the increasingly harrowing travails of Rita Iglehaut, a Garrison soldier trapped outside the wall, and her well-to-do childhood friend Mathias Kramer.

ATTACK ON TITAN: THE HARSH MISTRESS OF THE CITY Part 2

In this concluding half, Rita Iglehaut struggles to turn her isolated hometown into something of a city of its own. Her draconian methods, however, shock the residents, not least Mathias Kramer, her childhood friend.

ATTACK ON TITAN: END OF THE WORLD

In this novelization of the theatrical adaptation, the series' familiar setting, plot, and themes are reconfigured into a compact whole that is fully accessible to the uninitiated and strangely clarifying for fans.

The Seven Deadly Sins:
Seven Scars They Left Behind

Art by Nakaba Suzuki.

Published by Vertical, Inc., New York, 2017

Originally published in Japanese as
Shosetsu Nanatsu no Taizai—Gaiden—Karera ga Nokoshita Nanatsu no Kizuato.
Prologue, Chapters 1-3 translated by June Jungreis; Chapters 4-7,
Epilogue by Maria Maita-Keppeler.

This is a work of fiction.

ISBN: 978-1-945054-13-6

Manufactured in the United States of America

First Edition

Vertical, Inc.
451 Park Avenue South
7th Floor
New York, NY 10016
www.vertical-inc.com